The chapel was quite in keeping with the rest of the structure.

Garamond wondered if it had served as a chapel back in the time this had been a Vonyushar fortress. Perhaps the Vonyushar had laid the fruits of their military victories on the high altar.

Rather odd sculpture on the altar now, come to think of it. Must be one of Lord Roderick's personal touches. What saint would be carved to lie on the altar, her gown the colour of blood on the white and gold of the altar cloth?

It was Svarabakti upon the altar, in gown of garnet red, echoed by the brilliant cut garnets clasped around her throat. What an odd affectation, to lie on one's host's altar as if one were the dead carved on a tomb.

Dead.

Of course she was dead.

The living don't wear ornate fish knives plunged between their breasts...

Other Avon Books by
Atanielle Annyn Noël

THE DUCHESS OF KNEEDEEP

MURDER ON USHER'S PLANET

ATANIELLE ANNYN NOËL

AVON
PUBLISHERS OF BARD, CAMELOT, DISCUS AND FLARE BOOKS

AVON BOOKS
A division of
The Hearst Corporation
1790 Broadway
New York, New York 10019

Copyright © 1987 by Atanielle Annyn Noël
Cover illustration copyright © 1987 by Jill Bauman
Published by arrangement with the author
Library of Congress Catalog Card Number: 86-91000
ISBN: 0-380-75012-0

First Avon Printing: April 1987

Printed in the U.S.A.

K-R 10 9 8 7 6 5 4 3 2 1

For
Kevin Michael Rowland
the Poet in the Grotto
(probably drawing inspiration
from the lesser speckled frogfrond,
Ranaformis marginalia)

The belief . . . was connected . . . with the gray stones of the home of his forefathers. The conditions of the sentience had been here . . . fulfilled in the method of collocation of these stones—in the order of their arrangement, as well as in that of the many fungi which overspread them, and of the decayed trees which stood around—above all, in the long undisturbed endurance of this arrangement, and in its re-duplication in the still waters of the tarn.

"The Fall of the House of Usher"
EDGAR ALLAN POE

Contact

Being the Prologue, in which We Meet the
Cloak-and-Blaster Specialists

The sign on the door read:

The message was repeated in Shardé, although all the Shardé employees of Massicot Research could read and speak Anglisc. The door had a pressure-coded lock with a security override and a silent alarm. Gwen Gray, unauthorized, opened the door in an unobtrusive jiffy and entered, hastily followed by her cousin, Garamond.

"What did you do that for?" he spluttered.

They stood in a vast, sonorous, echoing darkness, loud with pulsing pumps, whining engines, and clicking servomechanisms.

Garamond was used to his cousin going where she shouldn't. They had formed a team and she was the lock expert, but he hadn't had any warning of this latest maneuver. The lunch lounge of Massicot Research, where they had been toying with fruit salad only a moment ago, had two perfectly good entrances for general use: a door to the kitchen with its exit leading to a handy alley, and restrooms with skylights giving access to the roof. Instead of making a normal escape through one of these, they stood in a nasty, dark place that seemed to lead nowhere—and where, Garamond realized unhappily, he could easily trip and be eaten by a fan belt.

"Wait a moment." Gwen activated her ring. It appeared to be an ordinary whistling green opal, but it had been fitted with a light that could produce anything from a thin, brilliant beam to a wide-range diffused glow. Gwen had designed it herself.

By this light, Garamond could see that they stood on a catwalk with similar walks above and below, linked by a maze of metal stairs. The immensity of the environmental plant serving the research center towered beside them toward the dim, distant ceiling and fell away below them in a dizzying perspective.

The vast banks of machinery hitched, twitched, breathed, and snorted to themselves.

With the coming of light, Garamond, as always, felt relieved. Their work often took them to such places, dashing recklessly as pursuer or pursued. But where was the foe?

Gwen whispered, "Did you see the man in the blue and white duralux blazer?"

Garamond shook his head.

"He was standing by the fountain, eating a mushroom sandwich."

"Which fountain?" Garamond returned with exasperation. "We've been three years in Kettlewharf, City of Fountains, as its council so modestly calls it, and you still consider a fountain to be a landmark."

Undismayed, Gwen elaborated. "By the fountain in the middle of the lunch lounge. Ostensibly not looking at us."

"So who is he? A member of the Shardé Separatist Movement? With Shardworld becoming a Commonwealth nation at month-end, they're rather thick on the ground." Garamond, rather proud of being abreast of current events, looked crestfallen at Gwen's shake of the head. "Or is he a hit man for the Fausta or a scout for the Green Hand or..." Garamond tried valiantly.

"He's the governor's agent. I'm advertising our considerable skills."

Advertising, Garamond realized, would be a good idea. The pair weren't on a job, and though they didn't currently lack wherewithal, they hadn't had a case for... well, too long for freelancers. They called themselves investigators, a good enough name for people who do a lucrative cloak-and-blaster business untrammeled by the red tape so dear to the authorities of the Oriel-Mossmarching Empire.

(Crimson micrographic tapes with tidy gilded-lead seals were de rigueur on official documents, and at the highest of high state events Empress Gloriana Gladiola proudly wore on her wrist a red ribbon and gold seal in honor of the Empire's bureaucratic traditions.)

"The governor? The Imperial Governor of the Province of Kettlewharf? Sir Cargyle Capricornucopia? He wants us?"

"One and the same," Gwen answered blithely. "But he doesn't know about us yet. He evidently needs investigators, though. Old Perugius wafted me a whisper that if we came to the Massicot's lunch lounge and impressed the governor's agent, we'd be the better for it." She fluffed her short, dark hair and her ring illuminated its chestnut highlights. Her animated gray eyes challenged Garamond over a nose-wrinkling smile. Her long, lean build looked well in whatever she wore, and Garamond enjoyed looking. After all, they were second cousins.

Garamond, still longer and leaner, might have looked sinister against the shadowy backdrop of generators and conduits but for his exuberant halo of dark blond curls. His large, brown eyes watched Gwen with more fascination than attention.

"Garamond, you can't be listening."

He dropped his glance sheepishly, put his head to one side, and mimed rapt attentiveness.

"The governor's agent is Gaust Kennes. I fancy that after our show with the door, his interest in us will increase considerably."

"And you set this up with Perugius?"

"To be perfectly accurate, dear old Perugius set it up with me. It's a good thing, too . . ."

Soundlessly a door opened at the far end of the catwalk. The Grays, with nowhere to hide, prepared for action or evasion.

A uniformed Shardé, obviously on routine patrol, immediately noticed the interlopers. He half crouched in a startle reflex, pineconelike scales spread, underfur bristling, hand poised over a stunner angled for a shot from the hip.

"Hello there." Garamond began with well-simulated embarrassment. "We were just having lunch . . ." He gestured with his head toward the lunch lounge while leering pleasantly at Gwen.

"Your ID, if you please," the guard asked with customary Shardé formality, standing at exaggerated attention with his blaster in hand and the sensitive tip of his tail out of harm's way. "It's so *dreadfully* unaesthetic behind the scenes, eh what? It would never do to permit simply *anyone* to see our unlovely inner workings, don't you know?"

"I say, we were at lunch." Presumably a Massicot employee could leave his ID in his jacket while he went to lunch, couldn't he?

"It has always been the fashion at Massicot to wear the ID at all times." The security guard licked the end of his nose thought-fully and stroked his full side-whiskers. (Whether the scales of Shardé are modified fur, or whether their fur is modified scales, has interested savants, human and Shardé, for some time.) "It really isn't customary to utilize off-limits areas for a spot of tickle-and-pat. I'm only a man of the guard, and hardly one to know the current trends, but I believe it's in vogue to murfle and nose rub in the roof garden."

The Shardé enjoyed his role to the full, looking down his slender, rufous-furred muzzle with the false self-deprecation of minor royalty or major vid personalities. "Please be so kind as to lock the door as you go. I *implore* you not to trespass again. It's simply *not* the done thing."

The Shardé, a stickler for fashion as only a Shardé can be, bowed to precisely the correct angle as the Grays departed. He perched on the railing, taking a firm grip with his prehensile tail, and wrote out his report.

I

Onesday

*In which the Grays Learn More,
Understand Less,
and Undertake a Mission of
Considerable Diplomatic Sensitivity*

1

The governor's agent, Gaust Kennes, by fiddling with a code left purposely breakable, could spy on the Grays' files through his information retrieval system. He felt equally at home hunched over the terminal or doing legwork, and he worked well under pressure. Right now, with Shardworld about to become a Commonwealth nation of the Oriel-Mossmarching Empire, with the particularly sensitive diplomatic disaster that could well doom any possibility of such a commonwealth, and with the governor's nubile daughter Muffin having disappeared, he had pressure enough.

He guessed from past experience that the governor would hold him personally at fault if matters weren't rectified. He knew that rectifying them was impossible. The governor chose his assistants for their ability to work miracles. And Gaust Kennes had a pressing personal interest in solving these considerable problems: Muffin. Lady Maudelaine, to those interested in the formalities —unlike herself.

On the previous day, Kennes had located Perugius, a perfectly bald little gent made up entirely of wrinkles, who could only be found at the right times by the right people. They met in the plaza of the Kettlewharf Import Center and sat on the rim of a fountain with the air of eccentric billionaires who had time to feed the bristlefish.

Kennes remembered the interview vividly.

"So you need yourself an investigator?" Perugius had hazarded, after a few ritual references to the weather and an exchange of identifying phrases.

Perugius favored Kennes with an omniscient smile. "I know a pair that can infiltrate and impersonate. I remember one afternoon they insinuated themselves right into a Glory-Be camp meeting, took up a collection, converted the heathen, won the cakewalk, and brought the false prophet Brother Brazenose in for questioning.

"That evening they attended His Excellency's ball in the governor's mansion, passed themselves off as the Marquis and Marchioness of Dimple , and talked the smallest of small talk while waiting to nab Frazier DuBois in the act of stealing lady Maudelain's legendary garnet necklace. He tried, they succeeded.

"By dawn, acting as warders at the Cloverhill Rehabilitation Facility, those two facilitated the breakout of one Underson for the Planetary Council of Ashpit, who couldn't proceed through proper channels. They got the Ashpit Ashen Star for courage under fire during the escape. They're like that."

"And they do all this out of an altruistic sense of public spirit?" Kennes preferred irony to direct inquiry.

"They come from a long line of antiquarians and historical researchers. Garamond's family has quite a fine antique business on Caladune. Gwen's people restore historical architecture. It's only a step from those types of work to detection and investigation."

Perugius smiled reminiscently, peering from under wrinkled eyelids with a deceptively mild innocence. "Garamond has a story that he used to play under a priceless Vonatun gateleg table in his grandfather's dining room. He was about eight years old when he discovered the Panbat of Oa's signature on the moulding of one of the gates. The family was ecstatic, and Garamond says his interest in investigation began with that episode. And Gwen is the one who hypothesized that the Panbat was under the table for the amusement of his famous collection of whitecats. That's the sort of people you'll be dealing with. Lovely folk."

Perugius had spoken in the offhand manner of a person who does not seriously expect to be believed, and Kennes had been careful not to believe him. Still, he took Perugius' advice to wait by the fountain in the lunch lounge at Massicot Research.

Now, sitting at his console, Kennes reviewed the Grays' files.

Under the date Twelvesday Foursmonth, '27, he found the record of a day's work:

Brazenose, "Brother" John Emmanuel—Prophet, false
DuBois, Frazier—Thief, jewel
Glory-Be Brotherhood Revivalist Popularians—Impersonation, conversion, probability theory of simple games
Maudelaine, Lady—Jewelry, recovery of
Underson, Partha-Kimsan—Cloverhill Facility, escape from; citation for courage during.

Either Perugius' story was true or a professionally elaborate fiction had been established. It didn't really matter which. Kennes went to call on the Grays in their office.

The office, on the floor below the Grays' rather bohemian spacious loft flat, itself appeared unconventional. They had panelled the walls in peacock-blue mirrors, giving the effect of an illusory underwater maze of doubled and redoubled offices, Kenneses, and Grays. Two workspaces of transparent duraplex had desk tops shimmering with an ornamental but functional display of current coded data. Kennes suspected that this type of information terminal, which had found favour some fifty years before, was about to revive. Kennes, who could never be considered a trendsetter, felt a pang of jealousy.

The three sat on transparent duraplex divans around a small table bearing a steaming pot of butterberry jaffa and three translucent Joramware cups. After a long, stocktaking silence, Kennes spoke. "I suppose you want to know what the job is."

Kennes seemed a colourless man—refined enough to be invited anywhere a second time, but with hardly enough character to be remembered when the invitation list was being written. This could be an asset, and he usually saw it as such. Except with Lady Maudelaine. By dint of skill, in lieu of personality, he had ensured his place as the governor's trusted overseer of personal affairs and of those official matters that would not flow freely in official channels.

Garamond began committing to memory one of Kennes' assets: his forgettable, faded beige good looks. It should be easy to impersonate a person whom no one really noticed.

The silence resumed. Not a hostile silence nor threatening, but delicately establishing that the Grays had the advantage.

"As you may know," Kennes admitted, "Perugius gave me your names. Rather unusual names, if I may say so. Archaic?"

"Oh, our fathers and grandfathers were antiquarians," Garamond explained with boyish enthusiasm. "Father rather fancied Old Earth's Arthurian legends. You'll know them from Bathebrush's opera, *The Lady of the Black Lagoon*. He named my brothers Gareth, Gaheris, Gawain, and Agravian straight from the stories, but he balked at calling his youngest after Mordred—a rotter and parricide—so I'm called after a Renaissance printer. Gwen's father wanted to call her Gwenevere, but her grandfather said Gwen was name enough."

"And I'm glad he did," Gwen seconded.

At this point, the mood had relaxed considerably.

"I am here representing the governor."

Garamond nodded.

"Perugius arranged for me to be at Massicot Research."

"They make a good mushroom sandwich," Gwen agreed.

"The governor could find a place for an expert investigator." Kennes smiled with studied blandness.

"We understood so." Garamond took a sip of jaffa.

"I saw you open the security door at Massicot. Can you open this?" The smile hardened perceptibly. Kennes activated the simulacra projector on his vambrace, a rather flashy model reaching nearly from wrist to elbow, with chromium dials and data display plates.

At once the Grays seemed to be within the multisensory simulacrum of a bleak and windswept moorland. As the outlines of the landscape blotted out their office, they rose and walked, seeming to climb an illusory hill of weathered stone and rank goose gorse. A monolithic mass of dark rock rose from the edge of an unhealthy-looking tarn of black water to dominate the skyline. The crag bore spiky projections that showed themselves, as the Grays came nearer, to be towers and turrets above a forbidding central hall. The huge structure—irregular, ancient, and occult in mood —might have been a fortress or a monastery or a neo-Gothic mansion of exaggerated proportions, but hardly a structure built by the native Shardé.

Buttresses, wings, towers, and outwalls had evidently been added to the edifice over a considerable period, but it presented an ominously coherent whole. The fact that it had windows, unseeing imbecilic slits set high under the slate eaves, seemed more alarming than if the walls had been blank.

Wind rattled in a fringe of rotting reeds at the lake edge. A stone-paved path led up the cliff overhanging the lake, past an unnaturally green and sprightly glade dotted with delicate saplings, to the foot of the structure.

Inevitably, thunder rumbled on cue.

The Grays trod a series of weathered stone stairs to reach a pair of green encrusted copper-sheathed doors ornamented with elaborate metal hinges and a monstrous lock.

The simulacrum faded, leaving the Grays just inside the door of their own office.

They returned to their seats, making a successful effort to appear nonchalant.

"You have heard, perhaps," Kennes began with a hint of malice, "of Lord Roderick Usher?"

Gwen glanced aside at Garamond, saw him looking particularly intelligent (as he usually did when he hadn't a ready answer), and replied, "Of course. The Special Ambassador from the Imperial Court. A noted eccentric who emulates some artist or poet of Old Earth's antique history."

"Actually," Kennes corrected, "he's recreating a character from a fable, a fantasia. If you take the case, I'll send you a disc of the pertinent literature."

"You're saying *he* lives in that vid show castle? I fancy it's almost too much in character."

"We are under the impression that Lord Roderick—" Kennes began, using the pronoun he favored when speaking for the governor.

"Of course, he's—" Garamond said brightly at the same time.

"Ah, under the impression?" Gwen tried to interrupt her cousin who, she realized by his innocent tone, was about to say something he shouldn't.

Kennes realized it too, and stopped to listen.

Blithely, Garamond continued. "He's called a Special Ambassador because he only ambasses when he wants to. Balls." Garamond cocked his head as if listening to himself. "I'm not being rustic," he explained with no noticeable embarrassment. "He only shows up at balls and garden parties and terribly sensitive Privy Council meetings at which he's not wanted and from which they can't eject him. I've heard he runs a form of artist's colony of terribly terribly sensitive, aesthetic souls, humans and Shardé and the odd offworlder, and the Imperial Court only calls him back to the Imperial capital when it can't help it."

"I'm afraid that's all too accurate an analysis." Kennes sighed. "We're under the impression that he has obtained a document of considerable diplomatic sensitivity. A handwritten, hand-signed-document, not an outprint, so we cannot take refuge in the excuse that the wording that we find so . . . sensitive could be machine error. A document he should never have seen, far less one that should be in his possession.

"With it"—Kennes poured himself a second cup of jaffa as he sought for appropriate wording—"with this document, Lord Roderick would be in a position to put considerable pressure on a number of parties. Diplomatic pressure," he added hurriedly.

Not in time to prevent Garamond from elaborating. "Ah, blackmail."

Kennes, who couldn't deny and mustn't agree, ignored the interruption and went on. "Consider that the ceremonies officially naming Shard to the Imperial Commonwealth will be taking place—I devoutly hope—at the end of the month. Sir Cargyle is having raving fantods. He's had his heart set on Shardworld entering the Commonwealth under his administration. After putting in seventeen years as governor on a colonial world that's gone through twelve governors of Kettlewharf, he couldn't bear letting a successor do the honors."

Kennes sighed, steepling his fingers. "To complicate matters, the Imperial Inspector General will be arriving on Foursday morning. Inspector General Carp is legendary for his thoroughness. He will hear anything there is to hear. Anything. As few people as know about this document, still he will hear. He's uncanny." Kennes paled, as if at memories of Carp's past exploits, and wiped his forehead and upper lip.

"It will be better for Carp," he summarized, "to hear about a crisis averted than to hear about a crisis."

"Ah." Garamond leaned back and drained his cup of jaffa. "So we are to avert a diplomatic crisis"—he looked innocently around his cup with one eye at Kennes, like a toddler playing peek-a-peek—"by insinuating ourselves among Lord Roderick's eccentric guests and finding one small parchment in a mansion the size of the Kettlewharf Import Center. And all before Foursday morning? This is Onesday, you know."

Kennes ran a hand resignedly over his lightly tanned brow and ruffled his receding, pale beige hair. He looked up and brightened a bit. "It's not all that small a parchment." He spread his arms in the manner of a storytelling fisherman, cocked an eyebrow at one hand, squinted at the other, and brought his hands ever so slightly closer together. "It's about that long, a purple-dyed parchment written in gold ink. Shouldn't be that hard to find."

"Shouldn't be that hard to guess who wrote it," Gwen said.

"I can't discuss that aspect," Kennes rejoined severely.

"I have the feeling that isn't the only aspect you aren't discussing. At the price the governor's office will be paying for our work, it's a shameful waste not to inform his investigators. Fully."

"Maybe I'm overestimating your abilities," Kennes said smoothly, his pale brown eyes expressionless and bland. "I really had ought to tell you, though, Lord Roderick has a profound nervous paranoia, a fear of assassination that would have made him a complete hermit if he hadn't an equally great desire to be surrounded by doting followers. He keeps guards posted, huge Kulmar warriors from Ashpit, at the entry gate and in the turrets. They have remarkable eyesight, Kulmars do, besides being great muscley hulks with a tribal tradition of absolute loyalty. Once you've passed them, *and* you've avoided the scrutiny of Lord Roderick and his numerous Kulmar servants, you're in."

"I see." Gwen's tapping foot belied her apparent unconcern. "That's all there is to it. A lost document, two people to find it, and there we are."

"There you are," Kennes echoed with false heartiness.

"There *we* are," Gwen agreed with emphasis, "but how did the letter get there?"

Kennes glanced at a dial on his vambrace and rose. "Later than I thought. Have to get back to the governor immediately." He found the Grays standing effortlessly and uncompromisingly between him and the door.

"Lord Roderick only leaves his mansion to attend balls and teas, garden parties and Privy Councils. There have been none of these in the last week, only meetings to do away with the worst of the disorganization of the planned Commonwealth Ceremonies. If the document is as secret as you suggest, he didn't come out simply to . . . obtain it. As I asked," Gwen demanded, "how did the letter get there?"

Kennes edged toward the door. Garamond edged toward Kennes. Gwen raised an eyebrow at her cousin, shook her head slightly, and asked, "It wouldn't have anything to do with the sudden disappearance of the governor's daughter, would it?" just as Garamond took a step backward.

Kennes lunged at the door, wrenched it open, and fled shamelessly.

2

Gwen caught Garamond by the shoulder as he was trying to decide whether to pursue Kennes or not. He turned to look at her with an expression that faded from anger to puzzlement to resignation. He stumped back to his duraplex divan, sat down with an emphasis that made the elegant structure creak complainingly, and remained, elbows on knees, chin on fists, staring with no particular interest at the jaffa pot.

Gwen strolled over to her workspace, sat gracefully, and scanned the desktop readout busily, coding in names from Kennes' account, and names he had left out of it. She didn't have to look up to see whether Garamond was still sulking. She had excellent peripheral vision. She also knew that moodiness was the only phenomenon that responded to the proverbial cure: If you ignore it, it will go away.

She had become interested in a listing of Lord Roderick's most recent known guests and had stopped consciously ignoring Garamond, when he sat upright and turned toward her, one arm stretched lazily along the back of the divan.

"I say, Gwen, old dear and clever creature, what was that all about?"

"For one thing, I'd fancy Kennes is in love with the boss's daughter."

"With the governor's own innocent little Muffin?" Garamond's sarcastic tone paid tribute to the diligence of journalists of several worlds in reporting what they called the lurid exploits of Lady Maudelaine.

"None other." Gwen crossed the room in a ripple of draperies and swung herself onto the opposite divan, her back against one armrest, her feet comfortably up on the other.

"What's this about Muffin's going missing? The press should be onto that like a greenbeak on a redworm."

"Spare me the colorful language." Gwen pressed her hand dramatically to her brow. "The official word is that Lady M. has sequestered herself at the Mountaine Aire Rejuvenation Clinique for her annual beautification. Mountaine Aire has better security than anything this side of the Empress' fu-dog kennels. Even I would think twice about trying to smuggle myself in. The press will prowl around the walls for a day or two, trying to eke news out of one another's madcap schemes to get in, and give up. But Lady M. isn't there at all."

"She's not?"

"She's not. Remember Marnina, that ginger-haired, overabundant dear who said she loved your 'b-b-big, b-b-brown ey-yi-yi-yi-eyes?' She's been working at Mountaine Aire, thanks to Perugius, and she mentioned that Lady M. simply isn't there, so the governor must be covering up for Muffin's latest indiscretion."

"And Lord Roderick is her current indiscretion?"

"I wouldn't have thought they had much in common, but so it seems. The peculiar parchment had been where the governor at least knew of it. The next we hear, the parchment and Muffin have vanished, and the letter is believed to be in Lord Roderick's hands."

"Letter? Kennes never called it a letter. And what was that about your knowing who might have written it?"

"It's a mere guess that it's a letter, but doesn't the thought of a purple-dyed parchment document written in gold ink strike a chord in your artistic soul?"

Garamond corrugated his brow, muttering, "Not Imperial. Fine rag papers for state occasions. The Quatermains write on silk, and the Ashpit natives use bark cloth and gall ink. The Ashpit Protectorate Treaty used the bark of six ash trees and eight gills of galls. Purple and gold. Purple and . . . Not the Shardé Native Chief? He's set a recent fashion in barbaric splendour, hasn't he?"

"He has. He assuredly has. And just in time to carry out the Commonwealth Ceremonies in a flourish of krummhorns and bagpipes, wreaths and garlands, and the closest his costumers can come to the fullest regalia of Imperial Rome."

"On good old Chief Hyoyot?"

Gwen shook her head in something like envy. "How a people who resemble a scrimmage of meter-tall pinecones can look so well in such a variety of clothing, I'll never know. Here"—she rose purposefully—"I'll drop word for Perugius to arrange . . .

arrangements, and we'll nip out to the governor's mansion and see what the governor has to say."

"The governor would never tell us about Lady Maudelaine." Garamond would as soon believe the sun, a pleasant orange luminary called Daystar, would turn back in its course.

With a toss of her head, Gwen assured him, "Oh, he'll talk. We're expert investigators, remember. And speaking of barbaric splendour, whatever did you think of Kennes' vambrace?"

Garamond glanced at his own wrist, where he wore the minimum of hardware on a 120-millimeter-wide band of expertly molded leather from a grunt hog *estancia* where he and Gwen had been of sub-rosa assistance. "Rather ostentatious for such a retiring type. If he were a man of action, I might think he used it as a weapon or wrist armor. To give him credit, his simulacrum projection is as good as any I've seen; but two data display plates, a double-sized communicator, and six multiplanetary chronometers —that's redundant. He even had a separate projector for flat vid imaging. Can you credit it?"

Gwen, with vague inclinations toward ostentation herself, but a dislike for chromium, merely sighed and began to bustle about in an aren't-you-ready-yet manner.

3

The governor's mansion stood in several acres of land-scaped grounds on the crest of Hotohimai Hill, overlooking the bay, the wharfside business district, and its lesser neighbors on the hill; the members of human and Shardé society and a few billionaires who almost mattered socially.

A high fence of ornamental wrought iron surrounded the mansion grounds, allowing a peep here and there through the shrubbery at the mansion itself, the formal gardens, the reflecting pool, the bathing pool, the summerhouse, and the governor's private Goff copse.

The governor, beefy of jowl, sandy of moustache and leonine mane, tall, stocky, and self-important, scooped and duffled his way around the Goff copse, coached and caddied by a mechanical AID. The Assistance Interface Device, a mirror-polished sphere less than a meter in diameter, floated at the governor's shoulder level.

In a deferential tone it advised, "I'd use a sand stick on that lie, m'lord." The AID proffered a polished, hooked rod on two of its four extensors.

"The divil I will," the governor muttered irritably, pulverizing a space of neatly raked beach sand on all sides of a small perforated Goff ball, which remained untouched throughout.

"If I may say so," the AID suggested, backing prudently out of range, "your stance has deteriorated and you'll never get anywhere using a dibble. You're just duffling sand onto the grass plat. I say," the AID added brightly as the governor brandished his dibble dangerously in its direction, "you seem to have visitors."

The Grays, decoratively dressed in scarlet tights and short black cloaks, had vaulted acrobatically over the wrought iron fence and now felt rather disappointed in not having had an audience. They seemed cheered at the sight of the governor barrelling toward them with dibble upraised, bellowing vague threats, while his AID bobbed along in the rear.

"I say, Your Excellency," Garamond greeted him, striking an attitude with hand so invitingly outstretched for shaking that the governor indeed shook it without thinking before he dropped it like a stingaree and stood his ground, breathing steamily.

"I say, Your Excellency," Garamond repeated, "I'm Garamond Gray, and this is my cousin Gwen. We're the investigators Gaust Kennes located to obtain the you-know-what from you-know-whom. We just popped by to mention a few things that Kennes forgot to mention to us."

"*You* want to tell *me* a few things?" The governor, uncertain whether to be concerned or insulted, opted for the latter. "You think you can tell me anything about this business? Young monkey-puzzles! A lot you know. You've got your work cut out for you. Get to it. I'm a busy man." He realized he was standing in a verdant thicket of his Goff copse and not beside his famous granitewood desk. "Have to keep fit," he added with spirit. "Do a round of Goff every afternoon."

"We can talk while you play, Your Excellency," Gwen suggested.

The governor looked the Grays up and down, checked the height of the Daystar over a twenty-meter scarlet-blossoming bombax tree, glanced with longing at his Goff ball in its much-scarred bed of silver sand, and, clucking to the Grays to follow him, loped back to the game.

This time he used the sand stick.

The ball flew merrily over a plantation of portly orange trees, coming to rest quite near the appropriate marker. The governor charged after it, knocking oranges topsy-turvy, and the Grays followed, dodging rolling fruit. "Fine hit, Your Excellency," Gwen applauded. "It's odd, isn't it, how a person will hit upon a thing perfectly one time and not another."

She paused while the AID gave the governor a wide-faced churinga and coached his stance. The governor swung, the churinga hummed with the swing, and the ball rolled effortlessly over the lip of the marker and into place.

"It's odd," Gwen repeated as the ball rose from its hole and hovered ready for the set stroke, "that Lord Roderick should have hit upon your daughter as the person to innocently bring him the Shardé Native Chief's compromising letter. Normally," she continued, as the governor swung round at her with eyebrows lowered furiously over pale blue eyes, "normally I can't see how he heard of it at all."

"What are you saying?" the governor bellowed. "What are you saying about my daughter on my property?"

Garamond stood by to prevent bodily harm. The AID cautiously removed the churinga from its master's hand.

"How can you object to what I say if Lady Maudelaine was the innocent tool of Lord Roderick? She's known to be a trifle ... suggestible. What would be more natural than that he should capitalize on her innocence, perhaps invite her to meet some of his guests, then ask her to pick up a certain document as a favour. Perhaps he even suggested that the document would be safer in her hands than in official ones, where it might be intercepted by the unscrupulous. Don't think too harshly of the girl."

Sir Cargyle, Provincial Governor of Kettlewharf, drew a hand slowly over his face: a bewildered, distraught gesture. "If I could only believe that was how it happened. . . . But as you said, how could Lord Roderick have known of the document unless my Muffin—"

"Oh, he's a clever old viper. He might have merely taken a chance of there being important papers about just before the Commonwealth Ceremony. If he'd simply called her up and said something to the effect of, 'You're just the person I need to bring in that document—urgent—fate of the Empire depends on it. Your old dad daren't mention it—as much as his life is worth if he says a word of it to you— or you to him. Oh, you know the one I mean, the one he and Kennes have been drawing long faces over.'"

Garamond, caught up in his cousin's imaginative efforts, added impulsively, "Then she says, 'Oh, you must mean the purple one,' and he says, 'Now, not another word. Get it here quick as you can. Leave a note that you've gone to some resort or Mountaine Aire or something. I've some fascinating people here you'll simply adore, so your time won't be wasted in the slightest.'"

"Do you really think it could be like that?" the governor asked with pathetic hope.

"Sure to be," Garamond agreed staunchly.

"I could see how it's possible." The governor accepted a dibble from his AID, swung, and loped after the ball as if, in his quandary, he took relief in any type of action. "When I found out she wasn't at Mountaine Aire," he panted as he ran, "and then got a gram from Lord Roderick stating in the most delicate terms that Muffin had brought him a document that she thought he would find of interest . . ." The governor scuffled under a frogfruit bush, discovered his ball in an unplayable position, tossed it over his shoulder, and turned and thwacked it as it fell. "He hinted that the document might be valuable to me—or to the press. With a story to go with it, 'Governor's Daughter Doubles as Diplomatic Messenger.' Some such rot as makes an honest man ready to—"

The ball bounded toward the water garden, and the three hurried in pursuit, the AID floating behind them, so as not to impede play. "Blustering Blackmailing Blaggard!" the governor roared, taking a vicious swipe at the ball as if he hoped that through some vudu transference Lord Roderick might feel the blow.

The ball leapt a pebble-lined stream, and the three followed— Garamond athletically, Gwen gracefully, Sir Cargyle furiously— to land improperly balanced on the farther side and be rescued at the critical instant by his AID.

"My little Muffin was twelve when Elaine—her mother, you know—died." The governor rootled through a stand of wart grass with his dibble. "I kept her here a year, but I felt like a spunk-root farmer trying to raise a thoroughbred racing doe. I sent her to a good school—the best school, if I may say so—and what good was that? The Sisters explained it when they sent her down for the last time—for climbing the fence and running off with an unsavoury young fellow," the governor confided with a glint of embarrassed pride: His daughter, whatever else she was, could not be called a stick-at-home old maid. "Explained that some girls listen to the Sisters and some girls listen to the other girls. Muffin was the second kind—but by thunder, I'll bet she told those girls a thing or two, herself."

"She seems to have led a rather exciting life," Garamond hazarded.

With a cry of joy, the governor reached into a tuft of grass and retrieved his ball, tossed it over his shoulder, swung, missed, and played it where it lay; where it lay, indeed, through his next two swings. Finally it spun away, and the governor, much relieved at no longer needing to harbour terrible suspicions concerning his daughter and the document, strolled after it, explaining with a tinge of admiration, even envy, "Muffin has always had a fascination with celebrities, cult leaders, and adventurous types in general. I say 'with,' as they seem just as fascinated by her. A lovely girl, and not so terribly rich—I know what you're thinking—that they should only be interested in her figure at the bank.

"She had hardly been home from school when she heard about the Ramuvishus in the East Arm. The ones who say each corporeal person is as a stone jar filled with the waters of life, which should be released to become one with the vast and limitless sea. You know the kind of seer-suckers I mean. She flew off with Ramu himself, one of those large-eyed soulful chaps that women seem to find so appealing. Can't see the attraction myself.

"In any event, she tired of it all soon enough. Didn't like having her perfect form compared with a jar. Escaped one night by climbing from a window on a length of unrolled turban." The governor drew breath. "Landed smack in the mud here," he ended abruptly, referring to his Goff ball.

"How do you propose I play this one?" He turned sourly to his AID. The ball indeed lay half buried in the muddy verge of the watercourse.

"I would recommend a backhand with the planche, m'lord." The AID tendered the required article.

"As I was saying," the governor continued, lining up the ball and waggling his posterior in the manner of a reed hen approaching her nest, "after that it was the Good Vibes Temple and Grill, then Sri Hamid Manuelito Big Sky, then that rakehelly pilot for the Fausta—Georgios—before he crashed on Brackenwater." He swacked the ball viciously and watched with satisfaction as it arced across the reflecting pool and the summerhouse in the direction of the next marker.

"Though why she should take an interest in Lord Roderick is more than I could fathom," the governor added, skirting the pool with an interested glance at the progress of his foetid lilies, one of which had just caught a large bronze-speckled water leaper.

Gwen hurried into the breach in Sir Cargyle's monologue. "When you mentioned celebrities, it reminded me—I happen to know that one of Lord Roderick's guests is the renowned vudu singer, Siphuncle."

The governor purpled around the jowls. "I should have known it would be something like that . . . that racketmonger, that cacophonic caterwauler, that gross, guitar-throttling incubus."

From across the garden the AID called brightly, "Hit right into the marker, m'lord. Doubled yesterday's score."

4

Lord Roderick Usher, born Lord Lionel Hapgood Pen-
dragon, second son of the Earl of Twilseydust and Strand, had
trained at a famous university, like his father before him, as a
member of the Foreign Service and a fastidiously riotous waster.
He spent as little time as possible in the company of his elder
brother, a strait laced dignitary in the Rickchucktarian Church.
When he had received his first appointment—as Assistant District Officer to the Malarial Islands on equatorial Elbe-Esque—
his parents did him the courtesy of dying spectacularly as their
light cruiser encountered a meteor shower. Left with sufficient
inheritance to live as he wished, he made convenient loans to
persons so situated that they saw fit to appoint him to a presti-
gious but undemanding ambassadorship on the colonial world of
Shard.

On his favorite worlds he had apartments and houses, neo-
Gothic in design, characterized by a semi-intellectual mess: furniture littered with papers, pens, penwipers, typers, and shelves
upon untidy shelves of many a quaint and curious volume of forgotten lore.

And he gave house parties.

He was giving one now, for an ill-assorted collection of artists
—he used the term as loosely as did they—at his Shardé manor,
and had gathered them metaphorically around his feet to hear his
wisdom.

They sat in the study, relaxing after dinner on the edge of a
snooze, lounging on a number of leather couches, armchairs, and
floor cushions, watching Lord Roderick as he spoke. Around
them the candle flames and the tapestries shifted and fretted
slightly in an evening draft from a high narrow window, while the
gargoylish grotesques in the carved and vaulted ceiling appeared
to wink and grimace in the dim light.

A gaggle of Shardé lay in abandoned attitudes on the floor,
some propped on pillows, some sprawled on their stomachs,
elbows on floor, chins in hands, tails up and drifting slightly with

the motion of the air. Yotu, the most notable of these, with his copper-coloured overlapping scales and wide matching side-whiskers, wore black and gold Zouave trousers and vest, revealing his handsome chest plates, foppishly laquered with clear scale polish. He sketched a delicate tracery down the margin of a scroll he had hand lettered with the ornate Shardé calligraphy for which he was famed.

His friend, ivory-blond Yin, watched him raptly with jade-green eyes, while her tail-tip clasped his fondly. She patted the underfur of her long muzzle into place between her scales with elegant whisks of long, velvet-furred fingers.

In an obscure corner behind an unlit fireplace lounged Dheloris. The vast blond woman—she might have been the caricature of a pastry-cook but was in fact the most noted player of the timballa flatstone drums—dandled in her silk-clad hammock of a lap a diminutive but lusty, bewhiskered rogue known for his mastery of indelicate verse.

Siphuncle, sandy-bearded vudu singer, celebrity of celebrities, lounged in the middle of a couch between Lady Maudelaine, frivolous in pink with short, carefully careless pale curls, and Svarabakti, his dark, sultry lead singer, whose ebony hair cascaded to her waist.

Lord Roderick lay back on his couch, propped up with tapestried pillows, a priceless blanket of Elbe-Esque embroidery drawn up over his knees. He turned his impressive profile to his audience, and with nervous, delicate fingers caressed the inlaywork of an exquisite Vonatun violin. He had never learned to play it, but lived in hope that someone would ask him to play, allowing him to decline with his ever-present excuse of shattered nerves.

"I don't fatigue you with my tale?" Usher asked in a low and beautifully modulated voice that would have been the fortune of a video-simulacrumion actor.

"Not in the slightest," Lady Maudelaine replied with over-bright assurance. "Please continue." She snuggled closer to Siphuncle, ignoring an angrily indrawn breath from Svarabakti on his other side.

Little ash-blond Yin reached up reassuringly to lick Lord Roderick on the hand with her prehensile, tubular tongue in that universal Shardé gesture combining greeting, consolation, inquiry, intimacy, and concern.

"When I was at university," Usher continued, "I knew that in artistic potential, in charismatic force, in temperament, I was unique, in no way like my fellows. The rowdy, boyish escapades they led meant nothing to me. The filching of the history mistress's garter, the crowning of the bust of the dean, before sunrise on commencement day, with an antique chamber pot—what were these to a true artist?"

Siphuncle suppressed a chuckle, and Fettle, the whiskery master of the limerique, whispered to Dheloris a brief explanation of these rites of university life—in verse.

"What were these to me, seeing my brilliant diplomatic career before me, my sensitive nerves already strained by overapplication to my studies?

"I took—what could be more natural—a mistress, a dark-eyed beauty of the tzigane-dancer type. She introduced me to her particular passion, the collecting of old books and codices. In one such she had found the account of a genius, morbidly sensitive, preternaturally creative, who could have been my prototype. I have made him, his name, his nature, everything but his unlikely end, which I should find no difficulty in avoiding . . ."

Lady Maudelaine, turning her face toward Siphuncle, thought she saw a glimmer of cunning touch Svarabakti's narrowed eyes.

"Yes, I made the Roderick Usher of the ancient poet's account the ideal of my aspirations. On that bleak evening when my mistress had slipped away from my rooms to leave me only the consolation of that volume of horrific romances, I read the tale that would be the turning point in my life."

Little Yin peered over the edge of Usher's sofa, exaggeratedly wide-eyed and attentive, her tail enwrapping the artist Yotu's ankle. Ever aware of her small, elegant features, she invested her gestures and expressions with conscious drama. "Ah!" she gasped with calculated timing, adding the final touch of suspense to Usher's tale. "And then?"

"Exhausted from my studies, I read, and seraphic phrases, fevered meters, delirious images rose up to enhance my already melancholy mood. In the crepuscular light, a greater glaucuous roke flew past my window, croaking thrice its guttural note, so in keeping with the tale's nightmarish theme that I took it as an omen.

"Later, during my work in the Malarial Isles, their miasmic atmosphere echoed and enflamed this sense of feverish genius, reverberating along my nerves until they strained to the point in which you see them now. In my travels I saw this mansion, this that the Vonyushar built as an outpost fortress of their empire before ours absorbed it. So perfectly it fit my concept of the brooding manse central to the poet's tale that I have made it my own; vaster, stronger, more sentient even than its prototype.

As if in answer, a beam creaked sharply, startling a dozing acrobat into a full flip, half twist, and automatic bow before he fully wakened. Beyond the walls thunder rumbled, echoing loud across the unmoving surface of the tarn.

As Lord Roderick recited certain passages of his favorite work, relating the thrilling atmosphere of doom and decay permeating the great house webbed with tendrils of fungus growths and towering into ominous and lightning-blanched clouds, Lady Maudelaine looked from Siphuncle to her host and back.

Siphuncle, slight of build, with expressive gold-flecked brown eyes and sandy-tawny hair and beard, neatly trimmed, had predatory and early-weathered features, marked by his active and successful pursuit of the primal musics of a savage world. But in his current surroundings, his affectation of a fist-sized graddy skull and a handful of iron juju beads bound around his head looked less like a tribal talisman than a decadent artificiality.

(Not that Siphuncle had anything against the needle-toothed, cross-eyed, arboreal graddies, considered pets or pests on several tropical worlds. He had simply adopted the practice of his mentors on tribal Tabu, who wore the skulls of late quadrupedal companions.)

"The reflection of this mansion's towers and donjons in the ebon waters of the tarn electrify my nerves," Usher continued, "with precisely the tremor of impending doom described by the master poet."

Having had Lord Roderick's favorite literature thrust upon her the first night of her stay, Maudelaine could see the similarities her host had found between the literary character and himself.

Lady Maudelaine traced his pale, noble features, the remarkable breadth of forehead, sensitive nostrils, large, feverishly lustrous eyes, and gossamer mass of perpetually disarrayed but picturesque dark hair—all the features of which he had become so vain.

"Thus it is," Usher continued, and Maudelaine detected in his voice a tremor seemingly feigned. "Thus it is that genius should live: in surroundings that echo the inmost nature of the soul. At times in solitude, at times surrounded with minds and spirits in sympathy, genius should commune with its own depths, or cast off the morbid shackles of philosophy in riotous carnival, festival, and masque. Thus genius lived before mankind hurtled past the stars on dangerous and futile, tediously modern quests." He touched pale fingertips to a bone white brow and sighed.

Lifting himself somewhat on his cushions, Lord Roderick added, "I have called you together for such a festival. Artists, geniuses from far worlds, soon Shard will, thanks in part to my earnest efforts, take a step toward its longed-for independence by becoming a part of the Commonwealth of Kindred Worlds illuminated by the wisdom and advice of our great Oriel-Mossmarching Empire.

"In preparation for that day, in celebration of the scintillating minds and barbaric splendor of the Shardé..." Lord Roderick inclined his head in graceful acknowledgment as his Shardé guests applauded with genteel enthusiasm, whiffling appreciatively through long, inquisitive noses. "... we will arrange a day of pageantry to augment the Commonwealth Celebrations in Kettlewharf. These will culminate when I present the Empress's personal representative, the Grand Panjandrum, with a particularly significant document." The smile that touched Lord Roderick's lips chilled Lady Maudelaine with an icy waft of apprehension.

"We must have dances, poems, pantomimes, Siphuncle's famed barbaric musics, singing"—Lord Roderick bowed to Svarabakti—"dancing, and such sports, all costumed in panoply fitting to the great day." Usher sat quite upright on his couch, forgetting his invalid nerves in his enthusiasm.

"Shall we wear black and crimson to show the solemnity of the event?" Lady Maudelaine attempted to flatter her host with a reference to his most favored colours.

"Ah." Svarabakti, on the opposite side of Siphuncle, stretched languorously, holding her thick sable hair in festoons at arm's length to each side, then allowing it to cascade back into place. Siphuncle stroked a wisping curl from her cheek. "Ah," she repeated, permitting her breast to rise noticeably with the breath, "just those colours that most suit our host—and myself. When I sing, I will need no lights and lasers to accent my music if I wear the colors which the governor's blond but pretty daughter has so thoughtfully suggested."

Lady Maudelaine, a young person of action, lunged across Siphuncle to give Svarabakti a ringing slap.

As Siphuncle tried to part the furious females, Lord Roderick leaned down to tap Yin on her white-plated shoulder. "I believe we need a change of air. Be a sweet thing and ring Borcubast to serve sherry in the library. With savory thin biscuits. The amontillado, of course."

5

Once back at their office, Garamond complained, "Why is it you know everything, and when you don't, you guess right every time?"

"Please don't, Gar." Gwen began to put a variety of small and useful items into a pair of packs. "No one's always right; you've seen the messes I've gotten in before."

"Like when you didn't figure the Marchioness of Blenny had poisoned herself." Garamond chuckled.

"Precisely," Gwen added shortly. "And if you weren't so sure you wouldn't understand things, you'd read more outprints and know everything I do. Goodness knows you have a better knowledge of objets d'art than anyone has a right to. I don't know a Shalima bronze from a Khimsan one, but you can pick out the individual artists, and their dates, and copies and forgeries—"

"Oh, don't try to jolly me. You know my papa was a dealer. I learned before I was old enough to know I was learning. Now if that damnable purple parchment were an antique, I could tell if it were a page of the original *Codex Aureaus,* or a later artist's affectation. But the way fashions change among the Shardé, keeping up with their current tastes is nearly impossible. What do you suppose it's all about, anyway?"

"What do you think? Here, check your blaster while you're at it." Gwen handed over a wickedly streamlined instrument of destruction.

"It can't have been anything in the ordinary, or the Shardé chief would have sent a trans with no hard copy. To commit it to purple and gold must mean it's of the deepest import, unless . . ."

"Unless?"

"Unless old Chief Hyoyot had taken to the plum brandy again. The use of purple brings it to mind, and it's his only real weakness—my stars and astrogators, he must be wild to get it back if he wrote it when in his cups. I wonder . . ."

"He hasn't any way to get to Lord Roderick's mansion," Gwen

reminded. "It has an unlisted trans code, unlisted portation coordinates, and it's not on the municipal survey file. I daresay the Peace Troops can code into the data somewhere, but Lord R. seems to have spent a good deal for his privacy."

"How do his guests get there?"

"I fancy he tells them to go to such and such a portation loop at a specific time, then beams them in himself. We're lucky we have old Perugius to see to us."

Garamond checked the charge on his Braun and Schneider vari-focus oscillating blaster, setting the safety and switching the test latch. Shortly, a high-pitched whine and a minute flashing light assured him that the charge was adequate. *Wouldn't hurt to take along a couple of extra charge clips,* he thought, and retrieved two from the underside of his desk, where he had taped them for safer-than-usual keeping.

"We'd better pop down and meet old Perugius," Gwen reminded.

They popped down.

Down, in this case, was a jaffa and sandwich shop located in the Kettlewharf Trade Center, now overfull of lesser employees discussing the state of the market in platinum, plumes, and peffle breeding. After wedging themselves into a booth between that of a minor broker still trying to warn a seedy-looking gentleman against investing in peffle futures, and a quartet of accountants planning their evening's revelry, the Grays ordered clear soup and cheese straws and waited.

At the appointed time Perugius arrived, all his wrinkles conspiring together to make a vast grin. "Ah, thought ye'd be here before me. Not so nimble on the old pins as once I was. And not so slow as some think me." He wriggled into the booth beside Gwen, gave her an appreciative leer, hitched at the knees of his drab tan coverall, and got down to business.

He pushed a pair of small tokens across the table to Garamond. "Precoded portation tokens," he explained. "It was only through my good connections with good connections of someone else that I learned there even *was* portage to the vicinity. To get the appropriate code, one of my gals had to do some pretty slick talking with a gal in the transportation department. If we'd gone through proper channels—and divilish narrow channels they be—we'd still be coding in requests to a couple dozen secretaries of secretaries for attention at the month-end reevaluation."

"We appreciate it, really we do," Gwen assured him. Garamond assured him even more with the gift of a treasury note.

"Ah, not particularly traceable, these notes. You're learning."

"We haven't learned why we're after what we're after," Garamond admitted, "but when we find anything useful, we'll let you know."

A harried-looking AID floated over to serve Perugius with lumphrey stew, which he ate with evident and audible enjoyment.

"Will there be portage to the manor itself?" Garamond asked, fishing a wilted egg-flower out of his soup and tasting it gingerly.

"Not exactly."

"How not exactly?"

"The portal opens at a crossroads leading into an area of moorlands with a few Shardé villages, a couple of large farmholdings, and a minor market town." Perugius stopped to carefully swab down his bowl with a bun. "Learned not to waste vittles on the sand march with Glangollen. Got left for dead after the Franji attacked, and had to crawl out of that hell pit blistered black, knowing every rock could hide a sniper. I learned the rudiments of my business in that sand, watching, watching, trusting no one . . .

"Ah, here's to better times." Perugius raised his mug of jaffa. "As I was saying, from the portal you go south by southwest on a cobbled road to a set of three marker stones. A path leads off there and follows a low ridge, drops through a thicket, and skirts the tarn to the causeway up to the manor gate. From the portal to the lake is about two kimiters—not a bad walk, even after dark. Asterzeei will have risen by sundown, nearly full, so you'll have light enough. What are you going as?"

Gwen toyed with her opal ring. "I had thought that if we were small-time tragedians making complaint that no one had heard of us, no one would ask us about ourselves for fear of boredom, and the guests would be pathetically happy to talk about themselves if we asked, rather than about us."

"Have any ideas about getting in?" Perugius looked up, a bright-eyed gnome, happily taking notes on anyone's discoveries. On the sand march, he had also learned not to waste ideas.

"Any number," Gwen evaded. "The guards, particularly the lookouts, are going to be a bore. I got a good look at the lock from Kennes' simulacrum. It's not keyed for the human hand."

"The place was a Vonyushar outpost," Perugius explained.

"Lord Roderick will have a simulacrum that keys to the lock, but you may not need such a thing." He grinned wickedly.

Gwen nodded. "I passed a lock keyed to an alien hand pattern on Ostrey Edvil," she reminded her listeners with a hint of boastfulness.

Garamond added brightly, "I remember. You broke your wrist and thumb in doing it."

"Wasn't it worth it?"

In answer, Garamond leaned across the narrow table and kissed her.

They were that sort of cousins.

The Grays returned to their flat and assembled an easily packed wardrobe of theatrical wear, tending toward flowing cloaks, pootock plumes, and the colours black and scarlet. Garamond transmitted a recording of the collected works of Lord Roderick's favorite author to his vambrace for listening and study as they walked the two kimiters to the manor. They draped their reversible cloaks gray side out over their moderately sized packs, and prepared to set off for the nearest portation loop.

"You do have the tokens still?" Gwen looked up sharply.

"I don't know why you can't trust me with the simplest responsibilities," Garamond grumbled. "Of course I—"

A resounding crash echoed in the Grays' office downstairs.

"What's up now?" Garamond muttered, and the two whisked down their minute spiral staircase to find Garamond's desk warped out of shape and a pall of acrid smoke settling over the office.

"A bomb. An old-fashioned, do-it-yourself bomb." Gwen shook her head. "Have they left the sign of the Green Hand or the Fausta Triple Serpent to tell us who did it?" She fanned the smoke ineffectually with her hand, then switched the exhaust unit of the air conditioner to highest speed.

Tendrils of smoke wafted ghostlike into the air vents and vanished, leaving only a clinging scent of seared plastics. With the air clear, the Grays could see that several of the blue-glass mirrors had shattered into seventy-seven years' worth of bad luck, Garamond's desk seat had partially melted, and a hair-thin wire that had not been there before reached from the underside of the desk to the ceiling.

"Watch out, Gar," Gwen warned, as her cousin crept stealthily on hands and knees and looked up at the underside of his desk.

"This wasn't here when we went out to meet Perugius," Garamond pointed out. "I know, because I reached under here for blaster charges. Look at it."

Gwen knelt and saw a smoking hemisphere the size of a jaffa cup, clinging limpetlike to the desk's undersurface.

"It's certainly not a professional job. Even if our agent was the only one to know when we were to go out to meet him, he would never hire such an ineffectual bomber."

"Gwen, do you really think Perugius would sell us out?"

"Not really, but we can't be too careful. On the other hand, anyone could have followed us. I say, is that wire a type of sensor? There are two of them, now that I look closer."

Garamond held his vambrace next to the wires and took a reading. "Something on the order of a seismograph. One wire checked whether we were walking about upstairs, the other whether anyone was here in the office. Very primitive, with a peculiar time delay on it. Some time after the bomber had left, it would go off if there was someone upstairs and no one in the office."

"I see—meant to warn us without harming us. How terribly thoughtful. I'll call our landlord and the decorator so they can have things in order when we get back, but we really mustn't delay much longer." She stepped to the less damaged console.

"True." Garamond, still on his knees under his desk, showed no sign of emerging. "There's something written here," he added, puzzled.

Gwen hurried her explanation to the decorator, whose aggrieved voice came over the console protestingly. "Again, Miss Gray? Again? If you're going to be bombed, blasted, and shot at, must you insist on mirrors and colours that show the smoke?"

Twisting acrobatically under the desk beside her cousin, Gwen looked at the smudged and blackened inscription. "Is it alien lettering, Gar?"

"No, I think . . . I think it's antique human, from Old Earth. What they called black letter when they didn't call it Gothic. Let's see . . . 'N-E-V-E . . .'" he spelled out. "Nevermore! How odd. What could it have to do with our current case? What have we done to Lord Roderick that we should never do again? He wouldn't have come here himself to set up this flamboyant warning. Would he?"

"No," Gwen agreed, reemerging, picking up her pack, and starting for the door. "Perhaps he sent one of his minions."

"His what? Oh." Garamond followed her. "Then again," he

puzzled aloud, "a more is a moorland. He predicts we'll never reach the mansion on the moorland. For all the good it will do, I'm going to lock the door on this shambles. On top of everything else, we can look forward to higher insurance premiums. We'd jolly well better go earn our fee."

6

"The trouble with the Empire," Fettle, the master of rude poesy, pointed out to those of Lord Roderick's guests who had not slipped away when the group moved to the library, "is that it takes itself too damn seriously."

The Shardé present all nodded avidly, while Lord Roderick, the representative of the Empire and one who took himself far more seriously than any mortal ever should, looked on silently with a strained expression of condescending amusement.

"And when all's said and done, what does the Empire accomplish? Tries to act the benevolent godmother to a vast horde who haven't been children for some time by any measure. Can't keep an eye on its own people and its own programs, can't mend its fences . . . and can't be overthrown."

"That," purred Svarabakti, who was leisurely braiding her thick, shadowy hair, "is because no group of more than nine people can govern themselves in full agreement for over two standard years. Look at the Fausta," she added airily.

Lord Roderick glanced at her with something like alarm.

Dheloris added another cushion to those on which she reclined, and tried to arrange her bulk for comfort. "How did a pretty thing like you come to learn anything of politics?" she asked petulantly.

"By rubbing up against ambassadors," Lady Maudelaine suggested.

"As far as the Fausta goes," Svarabakti added, ignoring her rival, "the Empire knows it hasn't got to throw the full weight of its navy against such a fragmented association of privateers. They'll burn themselves out with factionalism and in-fighting fast enough without any cost to the Imperial coffers."

Yin, lying with her ivory-plated tail twisted gently around Lord Roderick's ankle, had kept her head cocked toward one of the tapestries as if listening intently with her round, jug-handle ears. Lord Roderick, catching sight of her as he turned restlessly on his sofa, asked, "Do you hear something, little one?"

"Spirits, maybe." Her breathy voice nearly lisped on the sibilants. "I am *convinced* something is whispering in the spiral stairway behind your *fabulous* tapestry. I hear echoes of a positively *malefic* mind without a body . . . without footsteps."

"Stairway?" Lord Roderick leaped to his feet and lifted the edge of the arras. "There is no stairway. There is no door. You only heard the soft, uncertain rustling of the curtain. Listen. Outside, the wind is rising."

"If Your Lordship pleases, there is no stairway. No spirits." Yin became utterly absorbed in stroking the fringe of a tablecloth. "It is not the fashion to contradict one's host."

"Stairway?" Lord Roderick half whispered and began pressing feverishly at the stones behind the tapestry, as if he expected a door to open onto a secret passage peopled with ghosts. Fettle and Svarabakti rose to aid him, ranging farther and farther along the wall, pressing and twisting at various ornaments and bits of grotesque carving, to no avail.

"Why not call in old Borcubast," Siphuncle suggested. "If a butler doesn't know the house he keeps, what use is he to anyone?"

"Certainly," Usher agreed. "Be so kind as to ring."

When Borcubast arrived, a bent old man with a fringe of white hair reaching around the back of his head from ear to ear, and hanging, yarn-wrapped, halfway down his back, he bowed and, chuckling knowingly, asked, "What does m'lord desire?"

Lord Roderick raised an eyebrow at him quellingly and explained. "So, tell us where the door is, if you know," he finished.

Borcubast tottered over to the wall on incredibly bowed legs, put an ear to the stones, and listened with rapt attention.

"A lot that will do," Fettle whispered in an aside to Dheloris. "He's as deaf as a redworm."

Borcubast whipped around, his livery coat aflap. "Ain't neither. Can hear as well as the next fellow, but folks mumble so."

"The door, Borcubast? The stairway? The spirits?"

The old butler grinned impishly. "I should hope there was stairs, and sperrits too, but there ain't no door on this floor."

"Where, then?" Lord Roderick asked feverishly. "Be quick about it."

By this time everyone had gathered around the butler. Even Dheloris had climbed heavily to her feet with the aid of Fettle and

Yotu, and listened avidly. Borcubast looked around happily at his audience. "I hear tell as how this were a Vonyushar fortress in the old days. There's cattycombs down below lined with copper for the keepin' o' their armyments and explosives. And if any enemy took over one tower, though how they could is a mystery, the Vonyushar could get at them through secret stairs and passages that only they knew the use of. Leastwise, only they did—*then*," he added with heavy significance.

"Borcubast," Lord Roderick fumed impatiently, "if you know something about a hidden stairway beyond this wall, show us at once. No more of your nattering."

Borcubast bowed obsequiously, and led the way with his peculiar rolling shuffle. "I wouldn't have thought," he muttered audibly, "that His Lordship'd want all his guests to know the secrets of his house, but it's not thinkin' I'm paid to do, not so, but contrarywise."

The party hurried along behind him, across a high, chill hall lined with suits of Kulmar armour, through a seldom-used council chamber with the original round granitewood table still in place and in high polish, to the main staircase of this wing of the house.

Yin and Svarabakti each clung to one of Lord Roderick's arms. Yin, small for a Shardé, held on to keep up with the others, while Svarabakti seemed to help support her host, though perhaps pressing closer to him in the crowded halls than was absolutely necessary.

"Lord Roderick," Yin whispered, licking her nose thoughtfully as they descended the staircase and turned toward the kitchen and servants' wing, "what is your butler? He's not an ordinary human—not a descendant of Old Earth's First Families, I would say."

"No, you're quite right, Yin," Usher answered indulgently. "He's a Kulmar from Ashpit. Of human stock but divergently evolved, you know. I obtained him at the same time and through the same agency as my guards and sentries."

"A Kulmar warrior?" she asked, blinking as Borcubast turned on the lights of the kitchen, brighter far than in the other areas of the house. "The poor old thing was a warrior once?"

"That I was, missy." The butler had another of his embarrassing fits of clear overhearing. "That I was and proud of it. Ye'd never guess it now, and do ye know why? What everyone sees of us Kulmar is the musculyture. Mighty thews, they calls 'em. No one ever thinks what happens when a Kulmar outlives his calling to the millytary. Them mighty thews on a man too old to be active, they shrivels down to nothin' and them vast limbs twists and bends somethin' cruel without 'em. Stretch me out full length, and I'd be taller than Gyoyal, the door guard here. But I'll never be full length again 'til Poika takes my soul, and if I have any say in it, that final she-fate can take her time about it."

As he spoke, Borcubast dodged nimbly around vast butcher tables, racks of knives and remarkable instruments of the culinary art, fireplaces, and a microwave oven large enough to roast a whole ox, until he came to a low wooden door, much reinforced with copper and iron, under a wide pointed arch, webbed by the particular tendrils of fungus that cloaked the manor's exterior walls.

"There," Borcubast announced triumphantly. "In there is stairs enough and sperrits enough, and the stairs go on up a wee bit of a tower right past the li-berry, where Missy Yin was a-hearin' things."

"Have you the key?" Usher's command had less now of impatience than of vague apprehension.

"That I do. That I do. Use it day and night, and not an hour since." From his butler's ring he shone a small, coded beam of light onto the lock plate. The door creaked open reluctantly, and the old butler stood deferentially to one side. "There y'are, m'lord. Stairs enough an' sperrits enough." He chuckled lavishly.

Through the doorway the guests could see a narrow, stone spiral staircase twisting up around a central column into dense and web-clogged shadows. Beyond it, a broad corridor led down a handful of wide, neatly scrubbed steps to the forest of columns and arches that stretched away in vast and oppressive subterranean perspective—the wine cellar.

As Lord Roderick turned to speak sharply to his butler, a fragment of the cornice above the doorway arch gave way, smote Usher, and bounded to the polished stone floor where it shattered into gravel.

Usher staggered, leaned on Svarabakti's shoulder, clasped wildly at his throat, and collapsed with a febrile sigh to the floor.

7

Gwen and Garamond crossed Portleby Square, actually a circle ringed by administrative offices looking inward on one more fountain, and joined the early evening line of commuters waiting at the portation loop. Clouds began to gather, it became unpleasantly cool, and the line made little progress.

"We need portage just to get to the front of the line," Garamond muttered.

A drizzle began to fall but, as in the more advanced cities, dispersed before it reached the heads of the pedestrians. The weather shield around the portation loop seemed to be out of order. A cold, clinging mist settled on the waiting group, making the humans adjust their coat collars and the Shardé fluff out their pinecone scales and shudder to shake off the drops. Gwen and Garamond looked at one another and clasped hands.

A woman halfway up the line ahead of them said to her companion in loud and irritated tones, "This is absurd. Come. We'll go use the Fairmont exit." In the ironic way of lines, as soon as the most impatient person had left, it speeded up. The weather began to clear again.

The Grays entered the hatchway. The mechanism registered and returned their tokens. Seconds before they stepped into the loop itself, they heard a voice shouting, "Garamond! Gwen!"

They turned. Running up to them, pushing people aside unseeingly, came Gaust Kennes, his face flushed with exertion. "Here, you two! The governor has to see you at once," he gasped. "Daughter. Letter. Emergency. No time to lose."

People in line for portage began to mutter and shove. Kennes held them back as the Grays reemerged and raced away across the square. They passed the fountain at a light-footed run, twisted up an overgrown trail through an unfrequented end of a botanical garden, and came out on Hotohimai Hill into the last light of the setting Daystar.

"No matter when we get back to the loop," Garamond huffed, "we can't get to the Usher mansion before dark."

"Perugius said the moon will be bright enough for us to find our way."

"I don't like to work in the dark," Garamond muttered peevishly. "The moon will just make enough light that we'll have to work twice as hard to get past the sentries. Ah, here we are."

They halted at the ornamental gate of the governor's mansion, and rang the bell like civilized folk. A disembodied voice asked their names, numbers, and business, and allowed the gate to open after evaluating their answers.

The governor's mansion, a confection of white columns and white wrought iron scrolled balconies, emerged from its cloak of magnolia trees and toadplant hedges as the Grays ascended the white-cobbled walk. The door opened to them and an AID hovered in attendance.

"We must see the governor at once," Gwen explained. "Kennes sent us. Emergency."

The AID drifted unhurried down the central hall to the back of the house. "If you will just follow me, please. Had you come on any but the gravest business, His Excellency could not have seen you. This is his hour of relaxation after the rigours of his administrative day."

"I see," Garamond agreed knowingly. "All those weighty decisions exhaust a man of conscience. Whether to raise or lower the tariff on platinum and peffle nymphs, whether to tax sales of native bheer in country taverns, whether to use a sand stick or a dibble. Difficult life, that."

Difficult indeed," the AID replied, a twinkle in its optics. "Mastering one's stance *and* hitting the ball are a bit taxing for most humans. Here"—a door opened before the AID, giving onto the back garden—"you'll find the governor in the bathing pool."

"In his bathing pool," the AID repeated in particularly loud tones, giving a robust and scantily clad young woman time to dash from the pool into the summerhouse before the Grays could positively identify her.

The governor floated innocently on his back, apparently absorbed in keeping his large and well-modeled nose out of the water. "What ho? The Grays, is it? Ought to be under Usher's roof by now, with a jolly fine idea of where to find the what-you-call-em and how to get it back with the minimum of fuss. What's on your minds? Didn't come to ask me how to get there, I hope, as I haven't a clew."

The Daystar set, a series of minute pearl lights, came on throughout the garden and around the edge of the pool, and Gwen knelt at the poolside, leaning over perilously in an attempt to gain the governor's serious attention.

"Your Excellency," she began as the governor finally swam to the edge of the pool and balanced with arms crossed on the surrounding snowstone berm, "Kennes caught us just at the portation loop, telling us you had to talk to us urgently. About your daughter and the letter. What's happened?"

A slow grin spread across the governor's face. "Kennes, eh? Well, I'd say Kennes has happened. I didn't need to talk to you, but he wanted you to need to talk to me."

"Do you mean to say—" Gwen began angrily.

Garamond, having caught on quicker than usual, finished for her. "Good old Gaust Kennes waited until we keyed the portage with the Usher mansion coordinates. Then he sent us on a woozle hunt and transported before anyone else fed in other coordinates —and got there before us. Poor fellow. He's no expert—he'll be pacing around the walls for days. All this knight-errantry is pretty, but a great waste of time. Love of your daughter won't do him a bit of good without a practical knowledge of locks and human nature."

"Love of my daughter? Kennes after my little Muffin?" The governor heaved himself out of the water like a breaching dog whale, but the Grays had vanished.

Sir Cargyle, Provincial Governor, with the fate of the largest city on Shard in his hands, stalked off to his summerhouse, muttering furiously.

8

Gaust Kennes emerged from the portage on a high, windy moor and, faced by a crossroads, searched farther and farther down each road in turn looking for a clue. Daystar was near setting, stretching the shadows of three marker stones long across the wastes of wild grasses and goose gorse. From one road a narrow path led away past the marker stones. In the failing roseate light Kennes saw a golden spark in the dust but as he reached for it, it vanished. As he drew back, it reappeared. He sidled around for a better look at the phenomenon. His shadow eclipsed it, passed it, and it shone bright again. He leaned closer, carefully preventing his shadow from occulting the golden speck. He lifted it gingerly.

On his fingertip, he held a sequin.

Needing no further guidepost, he hurried down the path. When he reached the mansion, its oppressive atmosphere gave him a momentary qualm. Not being an imaginative person, he dismissed this as the result of fatigue. Unused to walking on the uneven surface of unpaved paths, and having lost his way several times in the unfamiliar moonlight, he found the sight of one yellow light gleaming high in a turret of the dark and brooding mass more cheering than otherwise.

He trudged up the causeway to the door overshadowed by its pointed arch, and pounded vigorously on the lock plate. When the massive Kulmar door wards greeted him with inarticulate grunts, Kennes announced brightly that he was the Venga Avest of Corbo, come with word of great import for the Imperial Special Ambassador.

After a moment of consideration the door wards remembered that Lord Roderick was indeed an ambassador, and rang for old Borcubast.

In the echoing, ill-lit entry hall, Kennes' courage began to waver under the tactful but firm grilling of the old butler, but he stuck to his story and didn't embroider it overmuch.

"I know ye says yer the Venga Avest of Corbo, an' I know ye says ye've got important word for his lordship," Borcubast repeated with growing impatience, "but what in thunder is a Venga Avest?"

"I can appreciate the care you take to protect your master from the attentions of unwelcome persons," Kennes replied politely. "I wish my AID would do as well for me. But you can't be expected to know all the ranks and titles of the highest officials of the temples and ashrams of the Empire, and it would be unseemly of me to chide you for not knowing immediately the privileges accorded to my person as Venga Avest. If you will simply announce me to Lord Roderick, he will know precisely who and what I am."

Kennes hoped fervently that it would be easier to fuddle the master than the butler.

"I can't announce ye to his lordship at this hour, Your Excellency," Borcubast protested.

At the words "Your Excellency," Kennes knew the butler had begun to weaken. "Nor in all decency can you ask me to wait here in the hall until your master wakes. You wouldn't ask that of a tradesman. It would be ill-natured of me to tell you what honours should be given the Venga Avest. The urgency of my mission has required such haste that I dared not delay to transmit to your master the time of my arrival, so I cannot in good faith complain that I was forced to walk several kimiters. Had I had the time to announce myself properly, the usual palanquin and eight bearers would have been sent, I have no doubt, and no doubt that you would have arranged it handsomely. But if I may not see your master now, I must speak with him first thing upon his arising. Surely in a house so well-appointed you must have a room where I may sleep, if not in the comfort and with the honours to which I am accustomed."

"Follow me, Your Excellency." The butler sighed with a shake of his head. "Follow me. I don't know when ye can see his lordship, what with his sad injury and all, but I'll see that a message goes to him as soon as he can deal with such things."

"Sad injury?" Kennes tried to disguise his joy at the thought that he could snoop in the mansion at will, with no interference from the master of the house. "Sad injury? Convey to Lord Roderick my thousand sorrows. What a selfish mortal I am, to be worrying myself about the lack of palanquins and incense and rosewater baths when my host lies swooning on his bed of pain. Whatever happened?"

The butler explained at length, proud to have so concerned and considerate an audience in no less than the Venga Avest of Corbo.

"What a fortunate escape!" Kennes exclaimed at the tale's end. "And what a sad irony that a man's own house should be the cause of his injury."

"'Twould be an irony," the butler replied darkly, leading the way up a wide sweeping stair, flambeau in hand, "if the house hadn't had a wee touch of help. Now ye tell me, Yer Excellency, how come, when the ladies bundles his lordship off to bed, me seein' he's well enough to walk up the stairs an' all, and I sweep up the broken stone and the nasty strings of them funguses, how come I find a bit of webwire among it all?"

"Webwire?" Kennes became suddenly and genuinely interested. "Tied in a boulter hitch or a half-serpent or some such?" he asked carelessly.

"Tied in a triple serpent, Yer Excellency, an' I needn't tell ye what that means. Somewheres in this house is an agent of them double-dealin', space-piratin' Fausta, Poika take their souls." He opened the door of a large and drafty bedroom and stopped on the threshold. "Or someone wants us to think so."

"What can you mean? Webwire is made especially for the Fausta by . . . never mind. What I mean is, none but Fausta would have it on them."

"That's as may be, but them who sells to one can sell to 'nother, as the dancin' girl said to the bishop. Here's the best room as is left, Yer Excellency. Tomarry we'll see that ye have a better."

Kennes stretched out comfortably in the huge, cold, canopied bed. The tapestries shifted and sighed around him, and from time to time he thought he heard something living wisp along the floor. The presence of a Fausta agent would complicate matters, he thought. He ought to plan . . .

The planning faded into a night-swollen daydream of fulfilled aspirations.

Kennes had first seen Lady Maudelaine at her coming-out ball. With her conventional unconvention, she had filled the invitation list with bohemian ne'er-do-wells and gaudy celebrities, while her father had added as many as he could of people who mattered. Graf Franz von und zu Fensterhalter had been on the latter list, and brought his righthand man in tow to remind him of people's names. The righthand man, Kennes, promptly forgot everything except that Lady Maudelaine, whom he had previously seen only on vid, looked infinitely more beautiful, stately, and unapproachable in the flesh.

Suddenly and overwhelmingly, for the first time in his dura-lux-clad and otherwise conservative existence, Kennes felt the quixotic madness of love at first sight.

He envisioned himself conquering galaxies and laying their tribute at Lady Maudelaine's feet. He saw himself rescuing her from bug-eyed monsters, berserk apefolk, and grasping octopods. He would bear her away to a world of flowers and bowers and sunsets and moonrises. But Lady Maudelaine hadn't seen it that way.

Kennes left Graf Fensterhalter's employ at the soonest respectable date. He did uncharacteristic part-time work to support his full-time job of watching Lady Maudelaine.

He became assistant-assistant makeup man for a Byronesque vid actor who carried Lady Maudelaine away for a twelve-day weekend and dropped her like an overripe lumpfruit.

He became butler for an unfastidious old fraud of a billionaire named Farquahar who tended to allow the motivator to malfunction on his star yacht when he took young ladies out comet racing.

He suffered the hells of an untitled man wanting a titled woman who preferred men of a lower station than his own.

He became a surveyor on an anthropological expedition on which no surveying was done. Lady Maudelaine had come along expecting to find the desert chieftains of Franji romantic. She strolled away from the campsite after sundown in the light of a golden desert moon, and Kennes scuttled cautiously behind. A Franji chieftain, intoxicated with puku root, carried her off to his tent. In proper vid-show fashion she swooned in his strong but tender grasp, though keeping one eye open so as not to miss anything.

Once in his tent, she discovered that he and it smelled, harboured a colony of itchy beetles, and had little resemblance to her romantic imaginings. She learned too that Franji chieftains have no understanding of the word *stop*.

Kennes rescued her.

It had been the opportunity he had been striving for. However, rather than worshipping at his feet, Lady Maudelaine got him a job as her father's agent. The job gave him plenty of opportunity to watch Lady Maudelaine, but as far as he could foresee, watch would be all he could do. He hugged his pillow restlessly, gave one more passing thought to purple parchments, Grays and Fausta agents, and fell into a troubled sleep.

9

Evening drew in. A darkness Usher could have called crepuscular blurred the shadows in Portleby Square. Few folk stood in line for portation. A rising wind blew spray sidelong from the fountain.

"I don't like working in the dark," Garamond repeated.

"We daren't wait. We've only two days," Gwen returned. She noted a shadowy grotesque haunting the fountainside, and waved welcomingly.

Perugius emerged from his lurking spot. "You two all right? Have your tokens? That Kennes outfoxed you, eh?"

"And we'll outfox him," Garamond put in shortly.

Gwen gave Perugius a brief kiss on his sunken cheek. "We'll be fine. Burn a muffin in the House of Szteblinas for us," she added lightly.

The Grays offered and retrieved their tokens, stepped together into the loop, and vanished.

They felt the familiar sensation of being impossibly and painlessly elongated from front to rear until, with a click as if their ears had popped, they were themselves again and somewhere else.

In this case they stood alone on a crossroads on a bleak moorland where wind poured over prickly shrubs and the red moon Asterzeel sent inadequate beams through rifts in leaden clouds. They felt isolated, cut off from any aid, and pleasantly excited.

Once they reached the Usher mansion, they crept circumspectly up to the least exposed side under cover of some overgrown goose gorse, its yellow-bloomed branches so high and leggy that they could inch along, bent double, under its prickly shelter. Once against the fortress walls themselves, they found themselves protected from the sentries' view by overhanging courses of stone at the tops of the walls. Only where towers stood out from the prevailing line of the walls could sentries have seen them, but with moderate caution the Grays remained out of sight.

"It's in a place like this," Garamond whispered nearly sound-lessly against his cousin's ear, "that we should be able to shoot a rope and hook over the walls and skim up with no problem at all, if it weren't for being so fussy about lookouts."

"Very thoughtless of Lord Roderick to be so untrusting," Gwen agreed. "Come along to the front gate and take a look."

"That's even less use, if Perugius is right about door guards and all."

"He's sure to be right, Gar, but at least they'll be on the inside. I say, I haven't seen any sign of old Kennes creeping around the perimeter. You don't suppose he got lost back at the crossroads?"

"I hope so, or he'll have put the sentries onto the fact there are people lurking about who shouldn't be."

The Grays edged cautiously along the lip of the cliff overlook-ing the tarn. They noted that here and there fragments of the walls above had fallen onto the vestigial path. They found the fact dis-comfiting.

Skirting a large tower under cover of dense cloud shadow, they reached the front entrance, a massive door deep under a tunnellike pointed arch. "I thought I noticed something promising about that lock plate," Gwen observed.

"You said it was keyed for Vonyushar manipulation." Gara-mond reminded. "Old Perugius said Lord Roderick probably uses a simulacrum to trigger it."

"Ah, but he doesn't. There's a smaller, secondary plate below, keyed for what Usher probably calls his aura."

"Ah, the flow of bodily heat and the essences of dermal oils," Garamond agreed unnecessarily.

"Precisely. Anyone with a thin, cold, moist hand can open it. I could do it with a dead bristlefish. But what good is that, with door guards?"

"We could stun 'em."

"Gar, we're not just nipping in to pilfer something. We're here for a good, long search. Guards don't take kindly to being stunned, and they're sure to complain. And I can't see talking our way in. Once we're in, we can tell Lord Roderick that we're friends of Siphuncle's, and tell Siphuncle that we're friends of Fettle's and so on, but servants are paid to be more discriminat-ing. If you tell them you're the Grand Panjandrum or a lyric opera tenor, they want to ask why Lord Roderick didn't give them spe-cial orders to welcome you with scattered posy petals and a fatted stag."

"So let's scoot on around and look for side doors."

"Yes. Let's."

They circled the structure with careful attention. Garamond found a hopeful-looking postern half-hidden by gorse and a wide buttress, but it proved to have been walled up on the inside. Somewhat later he noted a stairway that stopped a man's height from the ground and led up to what might be a low window. "Peculiar way to do stairs," he whispered with interest.

"A typical architectural conceit for this misbegotten mausoleum. Here, boost me up."

"Up you go, but from here it looks more like a niche than a window."

With Garamond's aid, Gwen scrambled up, noting that the stairs had a tendency to crumble and were slimed over with a particularly thick layer of the indigenous fungus. She reached the opening at the top, wedged herself into it, whispered, "Watch out," and tossed down a large stone, nearly smashing Garamond who had been looking up curiously to see which phenomenon he was to watch.

Gwen edged back down to the end of the stairway, and, perched there above Garamond's head, explained, "It's a niche now. It might have been a window once. It's walled up, but some of the stones are loose. The mortar inside, like the mortar on these stairs, is inferior to the rest and tends to crumble. I'd have another go at it, but I'd prefer to wait for some light."

"You would, now that you're here," Garamond hissed back. "I always said I didn't like working in the dark, and now I'm glad you see my point. How about some sleep?"

Gwen yawned avidly. "Righty-cheery-ho, in the words of the ancients," she said, and leapt lightly to the ground.

They inflated a tent in a nearby clump of gorse and bitterberry that grew up in the shelter between two large buttresses. Garamond set his vambrace to wake them at dawn. "You'll see," he remarked brightly. "Everything looks better in the morning."

II

Twosday

*In which Occur Death,
Madness,
and Decorative Revelry*

10

The Grays awoke slightly before dawn without the aid of the alarm on Garamond's vambrace. A moist, occulting fog, smelling of the early bloom of goose gorse, lay across the moor and washed halfway up the walls of the mansion. Here and there the mist parted to show towers and turrets outlined as if painted on the gray shot silk of the sky.

The Grays made a vagabond breakfast, deflated their tent back to pack size, and made another foray at the promising niche. Gwen found a few more loose stones by feel, discovering that mist and uncertain predawn light left the niche nearly as dark as before. She carried the stones gingerly, one by one, to the point where the stairs ended and handed them down to Garamond who placed them soundlessly on the turf below.

They listened for the voices or footsteps of sentries on the walls above, but heard only now and then the clink of metal, perhaps the decorative half-armour favoured by the Kulmar, perhaps the metal shank butts of lances stubbing on the stones.

As the last stars faded, a gaggle of gorse geese, fat and agile, swaggered in a line past them down to the edge of the tarn, giggling and gawping. As the geese settled down along the water's verge, nipping and twisting at the new growth of the sedges, a trumpet blew.

Far down at the great door, at the other end of the many-towered mansion, distant and delightful fanfares summoned. Bright notes bugled on the still air, marred by the few, flat brays of an inexpert trumpeteer, and echoed across the tarn.

Gwen and Garamond glanced at one another and Gwen leapt reluctantly down from her niche. With caution in the growing light, they crept along the faint trail hugging the base of the mansion on the landward side, taking what cover they could from shadows and shrubs, sedges and kedges, with their brilliant cloaks turned prudently gray side out.

"I really think we should stick to the niche," Gwen protested peevishly, as they edged across a space bare of cover.

"We weren't progressing too fast, and there's no knowing how thick the wall is there. Only the outer surface of the mortar is likely to be weathered, and we soon would have come to a stop," Garamond countered.

"Perhaps. Perhaps not. Perhaps we're on our way into the hands of the sentries. This looks like the type of fortress that would be sure to have a dungeon or two." On a belated bright note Gwen added, "Not that I couldn't get us out of a dungeon, but we can't risk the delay."

Garamond merely snorted.

The Grays took meager shelter beneath a copse of bare trees. From that point they could see the artificially verdant and sylvan meadow opposite the great door of the manor. At the sight, the two became convulsed with spasms of uncontrolled giggles.

The rising Daystar had just begun to silver the topmost towers with a tenuous daffodil light. Wisps of mist still wafted across the moors and stood in a nearly unbroken foam overtopping the waters of the tarn. On the emerald grass, rich with dew, four Shardé stood elaborately arrayed in black and scarlet, gold and silver, with every ruffle, braid, aiglet, and furbelow known to the Renaissance of Old Earth—as understood by Lord Roderick. With willowy gestures of their long and sleekly scaled limbs, with exaggerated puffings and poutings and inflations of their cheek pouches, they blew farandoles and fanfaronades on exquisitely etched post horns.

As used as the Grays had become, in their three years on Shard, to seeing, working with, and meeting socially with the Shardé, they found the image before them too ludicrous to be borne. The Shardé fads and fashions in dress and adornment were well-known, but the self-conscious vanity with which the trumpeteers wore their clownish garb overwhelmed the investigators with laughter. Besides, they had never noted the presence of cheek pouches; and to see them, each nearly the size of the bright-scaled solemn heads, bulging and pulsing and vibrating with the music, seemed one of nature's more surprising jests.

The trumpeting ended to leave wafts of echo jostling back from tower and tarn and moor. The trumpeteers—one brindle, one tortoiseshell, two sable black—bowed with stately reverence, their side whiskers deflated to normal jaunty tuffets.

The Grays, wiping their eyes, still weak with mirth, crept

forward, sheltering in the shadow of a huge buttress earthily scented by a thick growth of fungi. By dawn light they saw that funguslike growths enshrouded the manor with gossamer web-work as if with phantom vines, growing thickly on the lines of mortar in protected corners, its pale gray bands resembling shelf fungus but pleated into rich ruffles edged with rust-hued spores. From their lower surfaces the fungoids sprouted tendrils, soft and elastic to the touch, moving in the morning air like waterweed in a current. From eaves and overhangs the webs wafted restlessly in cascades several meters in length. Elsewhere they reached only as far as the frills of fungus below, though tentaclelike they stretched and contracted. They groped toward the stealthily skulking cousins, withdrew at their touch, rippled as with apprehension, and reached out tentatively once more.

The Daystar topped a moorland ridge toothed with dark stone, and shone full and flame coloured on the manor face. Reluctantly the mists receded, hugging closer to the surface of the tarn. Again the trumpeteers saluted and bowed, and from the great door issued a stream of revelers in a burst of music that welcomed dawn, evidently more gladsomely than they.

Some thirty people, human and Shardé and all festively garbed, paraded into the green, sunlit glade, welcomed by extravagant fanfaradonados of the pouch-swollen, cheek-puffing, elegant trumpeteers. The party, supressing yawns and blinking at the dawn light, trouped and danced. A spectacle of gold and silver, crimson and sable black, bearing garlands, scattering flower petals, they played music with expert and inexpert hands.

They frolicked and cavorted as merrily as the hour would allow, to the mingled clamor of panpipes, shawms, krummhorns, sackbuts, crwths, citterns, gitterns, tambours, tabors, and dudelsacks.

Gwen and Garamond crept yet closer to the buttressed corner of the great house, where they watched, screened by a thin thicket of bringlebush. Nowhere among the revelers did they spy Lord Roderick, Lady Maudelaine, Siphuncle, Kennes, nor any vestige of a gold and purple parchment.

Garamond craned cautiously through the bringle stems. "The door's still open."

Gwen sniffed. "What of it? Locked doors are safer than open ones. If we saw all the sentries out cavorting on the green, that would be another thing. Lord R. may be a silly old fop, but Kulmar sentries aren't likely to mistake one human for another— even less if Kennes has been poking around this vicinity."

"Oh, come on." Garamond drew back and doffed his cloak, turning it inside out like a pillowcase. The gray side vanished; when he settled it on his shoulders once more, it shone bravely in black and scarlet over his black bodysuit—perhaps not as vividly as the festal garb of the revelers, but not unlike it.

Gwen stubbornly remained in shadow gray.

"Come on," Garamond repeated. "You've always boasted of our ability to sneak and lurk and infiltrate. What is it? That niche?"

Gwen raised an eyebrow.

"I should have known. You have a fetish for doing things the hard way. All right, Gwen. If you want to tunnel through solid wall for a month, that's your choice. Just stand watch until I get in, that's all I ask, and you can go back and grub in that grimy little hole all you like."

Gwen nodded shortly, eyes narrowed, lips compressed.

Early mornings didn't find her in the best temper.

Out on the green the wind changed, and the music with it. Cold gusts rose from the west, and the Grays could see massive slate-blue thunderlofts rising behind the manor. The musicians began an elegant and extravagant march, some of them better than the others, with the dudelsack skirling and squealing insistently. The revelers formed themselves into a line, still holding their garlands and instruments proudly, though glancing with some apprehension at the sky.

The trees bowed gracefully; the trumpeteers did likewise and led the procession. As the celebrants came closer, the Grays could see that their festal finery had suffered from the dawn dance. Dew had soaked shoes, stockings, tights, and hems nearly to the knee, and stains of grass and earth showed on crimson cloth.

Gwen wondered cynically why so few arrangers of parades and pageantry took into account such realities as weather, mire, and pains wrought by unpracticed musicians.

"All right, cousin, come or stay." Garamond glanced back over his shoulder, saw that Gwen had made no following move, and with an eloquent shrug of his shoulders strode around the corner toward the revelers.

Gwen, finally prey to uncertainty, pressed forward a step, her fingers tightening on the butt of her blaster. She knew it would be of no use in rescuing her cousin from the door guards. Exasperated and uncertain, she edged one step back.

Garamond, with such a dexterous wriggle as he used to cut

into lines at cafeterias and portation hatches, found himself in the midst of the revelers, unprotested and even unnoticed.

A sudden chill gust bent the trees and flapped the cloaks and veils, skirts and ruffs, garlands and plumes of the revelers. A barrage of thunder crossed the sky. The revelers, aesthetic considerations forgotten, pressed forward into the doorway arch. The vast door closed sonorously, an echo of the thunder.

Alone outside, Gwen leaned back a moment against the cold, dank wall and wondered if she had made a mistake. She felt the soft, moist, cobweb texture of the fungus, smelled its richly rotten but not unpleasant scent: an earthy, leaf mould savour. She watched incuriously as the tendrils rippled faintly away from her touch.

She wrapped her cloak about her and—head held high against chill wind, a scatter of raindrops, and doubt—Gwen made her way cautiously back toward the niche.

11

Lord Roderick awoke to the excruciating sensations of pain from the stone that had struck him on the previous night and from the appalling irritation of the sounds of an inexpertly blown post horn. Feebly he pulled himself higher on a mass of pillows at the head of a canopy bed that more resembled an architectural folly than a piece of furniture. He lifted a pale and trembling hand to the bellpull and rang loudly and insistently for Borcubast.

After a goodly time the old butler arrived at Lord Roderick's bedside, puffing industriously from his climb up any number of flights of stairs, amazed still that his master's antiquarian tastes would not allow an in-house portage, and only one of those antique conveniences known as a lift—for luggage. "You rang, Your Lordship?"

"I did. What is that insane racket?" Usher, dank wisps of his hair clinging to his moistly fevered forehead, gestured toward the curtained window. "It cannot yet be dawn, but three madmen are playing at hornpipes, and a fourth is so painfully missing his notes as to bring on an increase of my fever."

"Now, then, Yer Lordship. In yer great pain ye probably forgot as how ye ordered a practice of dawn revelments for that there Commonwealth Cerrymony everyone keeps prattlin' on about. That's what Yer Lordship is a-hearin', dawn revelments, and loud and colorful as anythin' we ever had back at the Blood Brother House in my day, beggin' Yer Lordship's pardon."

A faint enthusiasm showed in Usher's eyes. "The revelry, of course," he muttered half to himself. "Though if the Empire had the laws it ought, I'd have that tooth-jarring trumpeteer hanged from the battlements with his horn around his neck. Oh, the agony it gives me to hear it."

"There, m'lord. Yer Lordship's sling is slipped from yer arm, like. That's what's painin' ye, like as not."

"No, don't touch it!" Usher drew back peevishly. "Call for Lady Maudelaine or Svarabakti. The ladies have a defter touch with such matters. And Siphuncle to help lift me to my couch by the window. I have a fancy to watch the revelry."

Borcubast tottered away, mumbling. "Nobility! All they want is spoiling and cosseting. A lot those ladies know about broken bones and broken heads, when his lordship could have a battle-trained Kulmar warrior—as I am proud to call myself—to treat his wounds. But no, his lordship wants pampering, not curing, and who am I to complain?"

As the white-haired butler reached the door Usher, whose sensitive and discriminating ears had taken in every word, asked after him innocently, "Borcubast, did you speak?"

"Not at all, m'lord. Not at all. Just clearin' my throat. That there nitre seepin' in the basements and dungeons is dreadful hard on the lungs, though it's not my place to say so."

"No, it's not." Usher concealed a smile and weakly waved the old man on his way.

Time passed in which Lord Roderick alternately dozed and groaned feebly, fascinated by a wealth of unpleasant bodily sensations that his fairly sheltered life had not previously afforded him.

He found this break in the monotony of always having his way quite entertaining.

He heard a bustle and upraised voices in the hall outside his room. An oath, a feminine scream—of rage, he fancied—and a ringing crash as of thrown crockery added to the morning's diversions. Usher felt a particular frustration at not being able to better see or hear the dispute, and was all the more pleased when the disputants burst into his room, still in full cry.

Out of sensitivity for their host, they attempted to hush their voices and to conceal themselves where the tapestry bed hangings obstructed his view while they brought their feelings under control.

To Usher's great delight, they did not succeed.

Svarabakti, whose singing voice had sensual, rounded, and remarkably flexible tones, automatically used this talent to enhance her argument. Siphuncle and Lady Maudelaine unconsciously modulated their tones as well, to make what might have been an ordinary, sordid quarrel take on operatic dignity and significance.

Svarabakti, in a full, menacing contralto, tolled forth. "I've asked you, and I'll ask until you tell me, why did you lock your door last night, after what I've done for you?" Usher turned slightly on his pillow to see that the singer wore her ebon hair in an upswept fantasia of coils and braids, while her shoulders rose bare above a floor-length chemise of garnet gauze edged with the daintiest gold picot embroidery.

"Why would you want to know?" Running his fingers through his sandy hair as if the operatic mood had overtaken his gestures, Siphuncle added, "What have you to do with me when you show such interest in the doggerel of that homunculus Fettle, and"—he lowered his voice, though not far enough—"in the Gothic ravings of our host." Siphuncle, his beard aggressively outthrust and his arms folded within the sleeves of a voluminous, black velvet robe, looked impressive enough that Lord Roderick wondered if it had been wise for him to dress his rival in period costume.

Lady Maudelaine, childlike in pearl pink silk, rubbed her shoulder against Siphuncle as if his pet. "I'm sorry, I thought she was only one of your singers. Vocal backgrounds are popular again these days—you can't get away from them. I hardly thought such an obvious type would *appeal* to you." Her voice rose in a shriek as she dodged wide-eyed behind one of the massive spiraled bedposts.

Svarabakti brandished a delicate but weighty bronze statuette.

"Now, Svari," Siphuncle began; but he quickly took cover at the sight of the singer's bloodthirsty expression.

"Again, Siphuncle, why did you lock me out?"

Usher noted that the bronze the singer held poised to throw depicted the mythological union of a winged woman and a rather exasperated-looking dragon. He didn't care in the least if it was broken but fervently hoped it wouldn't break anything else.

Siphuncle, muffled behind the bed hangings, returned, "What did you want to get in for, with so many other persons of interest? After all," he continued in a sardonic basso vibrato, "I can only further your career, make you a billionairess. I am untitled. If you wish a noble match, you must go elsewhere."

Lady Maudelaine, in a clear but untrained soprano, screamed melodically. "Oh! Oh no! What is that woman doing, that evil temptress, what is she doing with my garnets? She is wearing the garnet necklace, given me by my mother on her deathbed—" She paused for breath, clutched Siphuncle's arm, and whispered melodramatically, "She must die for this!"

She lunged at Svarabakti, tearing at the singer's hair. False raven strands and braids came away in Maudelaine's hands.

Svarabakti, her natural hair disheveled, half hanging to her waist, half still supported by false braids, pushed the furious blond aside. Transferring the statuette to her left hand, she casually unfastened the pretentious necklace of red stones she wore and tossed them derisively on the parquetry floor.

"Phaugh!" Svarabakti sneered, "what do I care for those baubles? Merely a plaything that I noticed on the dressing table"— she paused for emphasis—"in Siphuncle's room. In his room. Your garnets." She turned to face the guitarist, who stood, stern and forbidding, a shadow of midnight velvet.

"You," Svarabakti accused, her obsidian eyes blazing, "you brought me across the galaxy, you tore me from a burgeoning career with vain promises, and you brought me to this—face to face with the pallid brat of a provincial governor."

Before Maudelaine could draw breath, Svarabakti took a step closer, then another. "You"—she narrowed her eyes sorcerously at Siphuncle—"you ask why I wanted to come to your room?" She now gripped the statuette in both long-fingered hands. "I wanted to come to your bedside..." She advanced one more menacing step. "I wanted to tuck you in..." She moved yet closer. In a final contralto scream she bellowed, "And I wanted to sing your lullaby!"

She threw the statuette at her erstwhile lover with considerable vigor.

Siphuncle ducked.

Lady Maudelaine screamed, still high and melodiously.

The statuette struck a snowstone tabletop. The spines of the sculpted dragon embedded in the soft mineral, and the bronze quivered, giving off a note in perfect harmony with Maudelaine's screams.

"Bravo! Bravo! Bravissimo!" Lord Roderick, unable to applaud by reason of his sling, endeavored to clap with one hand. "Splendid! A marvelous, an aesthetic altercation. I am touched."

The two women, still breathing heavily in their unfeigned fury, ignored one another pointedly and turned to tend to their host.

Borcubast, who had waited shuddering in the hall, cleaning up the debris of a thrown water pitcher, edged around the door crabwise and into the room.

The women, neither acknowledging the other's presence, adjusted their host's sling, bathed his face, combed his hair, and dressed him in a robe of pomegranate-hued velvet, edged and lined in black watered silk.

Siphuncle and Borcubast attentively lifted him to his couch by the window, whence he could see the final measures of the revelers' dance. Entranced, he congratulated himself on the perfection (other than the performance of certain musicians) of the pageantry he had arranged. His room was too high for him to see the dingy and bemuddied shoes and hems of the dancers. He watched with some disappointment as they began to reassemble to return into the house.

At this point he noted that Borcubast had begun to fidget, rubbing his withered hands together uncertainly. He reluctantly turned his eyes from the window, missing Garamond's insinuation among the revelers. "Have you something to say?" he asked impatiently.

"Beggin' Yer Lordship's pardon, but it slipped out of my mind in the . . . in the . . ." He looked uncertainly at the combatants. "In my concern for Yer Lordship's health," he said with sudden inspiration. "But last night, after Yer Lordship was safe in bed with an ice pack and a sip of that there laudanum, up to the door comes who do ye guess? Why none other than His Excellency, the Venga Avest of Corbo. I put him in the Red Death Tappystry Room. He wanted to see ye as soon as convenient this morning."

"The Venga Avest, eh? Of Corbo? Of course." Lord Roderick puzzled, but came to no enlightenment. "I'll see him after breakfast. See that he gets what he wants. I would like lumpfruit nectar, white wafers, and coddled goose egg."

Usher glanced back out the window, trying to dismiss the problem of the mysterious Venga Avest. Of Corbo. The revelers had vanished, and though the trees nodded and sighed, only a scattering of raindrops fell. The clouds began to break up and the Daystar shone bleakly across the gorse-grown moors.

Lord Roderick Usher looked back at Borcubast accusingly. "The revelers should practice. There will be no more rain today. They should practice their dances, and the musicians must improve upon their performance. As soon as they have breakfasted, send them out for further practice. I must watch them. The Venga Avest must wait. Perhaps it would amuse him to watch from the edge of the green. Set out a seat for him. There. You may go."

12

Gaust Kennes awoke to the sound of distant fanfares and the insistent tick of a deathwatch beetle in the paneling at the head of his bed. *Someone's days of life are numbered,* he thought, remembering an ancient superstition dating from the days when timepieces had an audible heartbeat of their own.

Kennes had trained himself to awaken alert, responsible, and ready for (mild) action. Not for him were mornings of staggering about half blind and irritable, in search of the wash chamber or the jaffa spigot. He rose, anticipating the greater distance between the mattress and the floor in the Red Death Room of the Usher house than in his humble cubby in the governor's mansion. He not only knew where he was, he knew that he was there representing himself as the Venga Avest of Corbo. If someone had woken him by calling out, "Your Excellency!" he would have answered, "What is your wish?" and not "huh?"

Other than that, Kennes was hardly extraordinary. He washed, dressed in the long, black velvet robe that he found hanging in his wardrobe, and slipped out to explore. He discovered a high balcony with an excellent view of the revelers in the meadow. He noted that Lord Roderick and Lady Maudelaine were not among them, and terrible suspicions gnawed at his breast. He did not see the Grays, below him and concealed in the bringle thicket. He had spared them only a passing thought since waking.

He reflected on his mission and his sentiments for the governor's daughter, and discovered that his thoughts had taken on unfamiliar proportions. Vaster, sweeping, more grandiose, slightly patronizing, his imaginings touched upon the other players in the Case of the Purloined Parchment—as he saw it. He realized suddenly that he saw the world as a Venga Avest would, though there had never been a Venga Avest until he invented the title.

He enjoyed the sensation.

He said, "Venga Avest of Corbo," aloud to the rising sun, and the Daystar smiled upon him with greater glamour than when he had been simply the governor's agent, as important as that had seemed at the time. By rights, a provincial governor should bow down and abase himself before a Venga Avest, but Avest Kennes would not press the point.

Yet.

He noted, with mild disgust, the webs of rusty-spored fungus furring the outer surface of the balcony, and indeed, now that he noticed it, the entire exterior of the ancient fortress. In what might have been a mild disgust of their own, the fungus tendrils bent away from his touch.

He turned back inside and searched along the corridors, trying mentally to map the structure. He found it irregular in the extreme. Some rooms were high-ceilinged and spacious, as if corresponding to architectural fat years; others were low and misshapen, as if built with lean funds.

Kennes passed innumerable doors, one of granite wood embellished with spines, one in bronze cast with scenes from some forgotten mythology, one of iron bars, beyond which could be seen an awesome dark pit. Cold mouldering airs rose from it. Discomfited, Kennes departed with dignity.

Wherever he walked—in chambers cramped and narrow, airy and well-appointed, mouldering and dust marred, or lit with scented tapers and bright with bibelots and flowers—he saw no sign of either a purple parchment or Lady Maudelaine.

He heard the menacing mutters of thunder, heard the revelers retreat indoors, heard lady's maids and gentlemen's gentlemen pattering importantly about. He wondered where Lord Roderick had obtained so many human servants in an age so dependent upon the mechanical AID, then realized that the manners and economies of the worlds of the Empire offered a wide variety of luxuries indeed.

It might still be possible to purchase human slaves, he thought, first with shock, then with calculation as to whether such a retinue would enhance his standing as Venga Avest. He concluded that the responsibility for slaves, as for a stable of fine hunting-stags, might be an inconvenience.

He returned from a tower that he had been examining for signs of an ornamented cylindrical official scroll case, and lurked in a niche on one of the lower floors. When he saw Borcubast pottering along toward the Red Death Room, he gracefully intercepted him.

"Ah! Borcubast, is it not? Were you about to call for me?" Kennes thought it unwise to explain why he had emerged portentously from a niche. He would allow the butler to suppose this was one of the things Venga Avests, of Corbo or otherwise, tended to find appropriate.

"Yer Excellency!" Borcubast bowed extravagantly. "I came to announce breakfast. Will ye take yer meal with the other guests or in yer room? Lord Roderick assured me that ye were to have anything that ye wished."

Kennes' first impulse was to ask for a tray in his room; however, remembering that he *was* the Venga Avest, after all, he reminded, "I had asked to see Lord Roderick as soon as possible this morning. Will he be at breakfast? When can I see him?"

Borcubast looked with concentration at his own curly-toed shoes of black-lacquered leather. "His lordship is still groanful sore, Yer Excellency. He'll be takin' breakfast in his room, an' he's not fit for conferencin' an' such until he's fed. If then."

"A pity." Kennes shook his head with philosophical forgiveness. "Were it not Lord Roderick, and had he not met with such an unfortunate accident, I would have no choice but to ascend to his room and bring him my message with no further delay."

Borcubast began to look alarmed.

"But under the circumstances, it is better that Lord Roderick be somewhat recovered, that he may give the fullest attention to the matters of policy and pomp that I bring to him. Now, as to my breakfast, would it be possible for me to obtain creamed cormorant eggs? With the yolks unbroken, of course."

Borcubast brightened. "What a mercy! What a mercy, Yer Excellency! The kitchen maid as gathers the goose eggs fer his lordship, what do ye suppose she found out on that little eyot down by the dead bristletree?"

"Indeed?" Kennes hastened the tale with cool interest.

"Why, a cormorant nest, sir—Yer Excellency, I should say—an' she can only just jump to that there eyot. Many a time I've heard her say—"

"Enough." Kennes waved him ahead down the corridor with gentle reproof. "It is one thing to find an egg, another to cook it to ideal consistency."

During his morning explorations Kennes had passed the pantry and heard the girl describing her marvelous fortune, but he saw no reason to mention this.

* * *

The breakfast room at the Usher mansion had none of the heavy formality of the great banquet hall in which the evening meal was taken amid ceremonial elegance or riotous revelings. Here, a few window slits admitted the eastern light, and a great many tapers and torches and banked flowers in white, gold, and rose gave the impression of light and freshness missing in much of the house.

The guests displayed equal informality. Breakfast had been set out as a buffet, and people wandered around the room or perched on hassocks or reclined on couches or even returned to their own chambers with dainty plates of this and that, in a manner that Kennes considered quite irregular and, as Venga Avest, found nearly scandalous.

Yotu, his fox red side-whiskers neatly brushed and his tail emerging negligently from a pair of turquoise trousers of Mogul cut, caught Kennes' attention. He seemed to behave rather secretively, facing into a corner, flourishing an ultrafine brush in one hand and a fork in the other. On closer inspection, however, he was merely lettering a signboard for his door with the most elaborate arabesques of the highest Shardé calligraphy, reading, Do Not Disturb, while his other hand, independently, fed him with mushrooms dipped in sweet cream and hearty wedges of gorse goose liver pâté served in twists of red taro skin.

Kennes looked up from this talented exhibition to see Lady Maudelaine enter the room, fetchingly gowned in pink. She showed signs of exasperation—not unusual for her in the morning—and unconsciously twisted her necklace of red stones.

She did not see Kennes.

From the service door Borcubast, flanked by two liveried footmen, ushered in no lesser personage than the cook: a vast, placid Kulmar woman with a blond braid reaching to her knees, her cheeks and nose glowing red from the ovens. She bore a lordly dish of exquisitely arranged cormorant eggs—yolks unbroken—blended to perfection with the cream sauce, bordered with pastry puffs, bristlefish roe, and water leaves.

Perhaps louder than absolutely necessary, the butler announced, "Yer Excellency, yer breakfast is served."

The other guests, nibbling at bits of toast while suppressing yawns or methodically stuffing themselves with delicacies, now looked up to see what "Excellency" had joined them. They saw a man of pleasant-but-forgettable features, lightly tanned, with beige hair and pale brown eyes—ah, but how he held himself. What authority gave his stance, his gestures, his nod, the lift of his eyebrow, a significance greater than those of other mortals.

A celebrity among celebrities, Kennes found himself announced to artists, actors, entertainers whose very names would have given him palpitations as the governor's agent, but who made way for him (though with a normal amount of whispers and mutters) at the butler's mysterious introduction.

"Ah." Fettle elbowed Dheloris' ribs, making her choke over a gargantuan sweet bun. "The Venga Avest. Of Corbo. How odd. I wonder what brings him here." Fettle's muse moved him to add,

> "The Venga, at breakfast on Shard
> Found his eggs had been flavoured with lard.
>   It's not that they stick—"

Mercifully, he was interrupted.

Lady Maudelaine, who had only glanced up from her broodings at Borcubast's announcement, glided angrily over to the butler, examining him as if he had taken leave of his senses. "Did you say that man was the Venga Avest? Of Corbo? Why is he here?" And moved by growing uncertainties about a parchment her host had asked, as a favour, that she convey to him herself, she added under her breath, "What have I done?"

Kennes feigned surprise. "How pleasant! Lady Maudelaine, I believe. The governor's daughter from Kettlewharf. Please, please consider me only as an Imperial messenger to Lord Roderick. As for what you have done, all mortals are transgressors. Outside the sacred precincts of Corbo, I can neither grant absolution nor prescribe penance. I will only suggest to transgressors to do such acts of penitence that their consciences make manifest."

These last sentences were uttered with a certain added significance, and the glances that passed between Lady Maudelaine and her father's agent carried a conversation of their own.

Kennes' cocked eyebrow questioned. Maudelaine lowered her chin, half sulky, half ashamed. The turn of Kennes' head recommended a solution. Maudelaine's sigh acquiesced.

"Your Excellency." She held out both her hands to him and bowed her head slightly as he took them gravely. "Forgive my impetuous questions. I should never have thought to burden you with my concerns when you are weighted down with matters of state, conferences, documents"—she pressed his hand slightly and he signalled back—"matters only for such as my father and Lord Roderick . . ."

"And even the Empress herself," Kennes finished. "Oh, yes, great matters are afoot, beyond even Shard's coming elevation to the Commonwealth. But other matters are pressing. Even with our host's excellent hot plate, eggs cannot wait forever. Excuse me, but I fear that a few more moments delay will cause a certain coarsening of the albumen that would not be forgiven by our so excellent cook."

Lady Maudelaine withdrew her hands with a reluctance that Kennes found gratifying but inexplicable. She would not, he felt assured, mention his other—his past?—identity until she knew more about the parchment and what it meant to her father. He turned his attention to the patiently waiting cook.

By nature an even-tempered woman, the cook felt a certain superiority to the temperamental clabber-de-clawing that tended to occur in this eccentric household. If many of the staff hadn't been her countrymen, she tended to say with a certain austerity after partaking of much-sugared jaffa, no credit nor coin nor appreciation of her cooking would keep her in a place so given over to wauler-youping.

But in the Venga Avest she saw a perfect gentleman who knew good food and gave proper priority to eggs and cream sauce, even when he had a lovely—if spoiled and whinesome—young lady a-holding his hands. With a sigh of properly disciplined joy, she handed over the dish for a footman to place before His Excellency.

13

Gwen edged along the base of the mansion. She heard nothing but the wind sighing in the turrets above her and intermittent thunder becoming more and more distant. The clouds drew off slightly but the air remained oppressive.

Without warning, something wrapped itself securely around her ankle. She drew back, but it followed. Gwen looked down to find herself entangled in a length of webwire. Not a snare or a trap, but simply a discarded strand.

Of course, she thought, *one doesn't simply find webwire lying about everywhere like wrappers and string. Webwire means Fausta agents about and no one else.* She looked up to see what window it might have fallen from and noted two or three possibilities. Or it might have been dropped by someone skirting the building's edge, as she was.

She tried to think how the Fausta could fit into the matter of a stolen parchment. Lord R. could be going to sell it to them. They might have discovered it and be trying to blackmail him into giving it up. She wondered why Usher had stolen it in the first place. If, as Kennes suggested, he was blackmailing the governor and possibly the Shardé Native Chief, how could it be for money when he seemed so inexhaustably wealthy?

But then people often behaved as if they were wealthy so people wouldn't know they no longer were.

Fausta, she thought.

Odd.

She coiled up the bit of webwire neatly and concealed it in her pack.

Reaching the half-a-stairway, she discovered that it had been far easier to get up to the point where the steps started when she had had Garamond along to give her a boost.

In the daylight, the niche at the top looked shallower and less mysterious, and the stonework at the back looked better mortared and more unyielding than they had in the dark.

She wondered if she had not only made a mistake but also a remarkably silly one.

By dint of some ambitious acrobatics she levered herself onto the end of the stairway. Climbing up into the niche, she found there were still a number of somewhat loose stones, and applied herself to their removal. She pried out a rather large specimen and dropped it into the undergrowth below. Branches cracked and the stone hit the moss below with an awesome thump.

Gwen backed hurriedly into the niche, expecting to be set upon by implacable sentries and carried off to dungeons for unspeakable tortures. She reviewed several mental disciplines for withstanding tortures, to the point that she felt nearly disappointed when no sentries arrived.

She removed another stone to discover that it had been sheltering a family of musk beetles. She wafted them humanely down into the bushes with the lightest possible of blasts from her blaster, then retired to the far end of the stairway while the musk aired from the niche.

She returned and levered out another stone. And another.

She discovered the particular setting for her blaster that best disintegrated mortar from around stones with the least inconvenience from flying spinters or dust.

She attempted to let down the stones in a cradle of webwire but found that the wire, so well suited to the rigours of space, tended to lose its flexibility at the least convenient moments in planetside atmosphere. For this reason traditional spacefarers, when they used wire at all, used a more expensive composition that could be used planetside as well. But then, they didn't have to immobilize captured vessels and lash them to their own hulls, a habit the Fausta may have adapted from the ancient whalers.

A framework of lithe bitterberry saplings was the best Gwen could invent for the least audible disposal of stones.

She had just noticed that her hands were becoming stained by reddish, pungent bitterberry resin when she froze in heart-stopping paralysis at the sound, below, of a throat being cleared.

"You, up there," came a male human voice, most certainly not that of Garamond. With acid sarcasm, it continued, "May I be of assistance?"

14

U pon entering the mansion, Garamond had followed un-
obtrusively in the wake of a knot of revelers, listening avidly.

"How tedious, Kelesophos, dearest. I'm ready to split my
jaws with yawning." A young woman with enormous eyes and a
garland of limp posies in her strawberry blond hair leaned, fash-
ionably world-weary, on a companion's arm. "Up before dawn,
with my maid trying to dress me with her eyes shut. What havoc.
All this planning, and when we did finally have sunrise rehearsal,
poor Lord Roddy wasn't even there to see it."

"But Patrice, didn't you hear? Some Fausta set a trip-trap for
him in the wine cellar, and he only escaped with his life. A gar-
goyle struck him on the head and he's lying delirious with brain
fever. If poor old Borcubast hadn't pulled him back just in
time . . ."

"No, not as I heard it," drawled a Shardé whose scarlet
snouter wool cloak contrasted with his own silvery olive scales. "I
heard that old Borcubast ponged him on the cranial dome with a
magnum of Chateau Vonatu ought-three for an imagined slight.
Very unfashionable behavior, that. They took him to the dungeons
and he's collapsed into a coma."

"Dear Hyota-ya, your almost impeccable Anglisc still has few
flaws in the pronouns." Patrice sighed, arranging her garland. "I
suppose you mean the butler's in the dungeons and Lord Roddy's
in a coma? How tragic! That is serious, isn't it?" She gazed up at
Kelesophos as if expecting him to make an expert medical pronouncement.

Kelesophos, a much-befreckled musician with a dudelsack
negligently cradled on one arm and Patrice on the other, cleared
his throat knowledgably. "Actually, if you look, you'll see our
butler free, unshackled, undungeoned, apparently addressing
some sharp remarks to that odd young footman who tends to get
his thumb into my soup."

"Does he, eh?" Hyota-ya delicately polished his tail with a

lace-edged hankerchee. "The one named Brennu? I fancy his attention wanders toward one of the maids."

Garamond Gray, emerging with the three revelers into the light and airy room where Borcubast held sway over a collection of sleepy footmen, felt engulfed in a wave of savoury scents. Cinnamon, bitterbark, marjoram, and sweetweed all reminded him that his tentside breakfast had been small, simple, and quite long ago.

He had just abstracted a sweet muffin in a lace napkin when Borcubast announced, "Your Excellency, your breakfast is served." Garamond glanced up to see that the black velvet clad Excellency smiling condescendingly upon the cook could only be Gaust Kennes representing himself as someone else.

Garamond had slipped into the shadow of an elaborately inlaid cabinet as Lady Maudelaine entered. He watched as she and Kennes came to some inexplicable understanding. He heard enough to know that Kennes was playing the Venga Avest of Corbo, and that the governor's daughter would not reveal him.

Yet.

Garamond wondered why not. He allowed twin Kulmar serving maids to fill him a cup of jaffa, and, still half concealed, breakfasted while listening avidly.

A moment later all heads turned, even that of Kennes, though with the reluctant, incurious motion suitable for a Venga Avest with a mind above such matters. Where Lady Maudelaine had been the center of male glances of interest and female affectations of unconcern—masking much conjecture and not a little envy— the woman who entered now caused a number of jaws to drop.

Her hair fell in a dark, undulating curtain from a crown of braids. Her form, concealed in a drift of garnet gauze, still signalled its siren sensuality with every motion. Her wide, dark eyes narrowed now with a wicked lift of the lower lids. Her expressive hands clutched clawlike, and she looked quite ready to commit murder.

"Svarabakti, dearest!" a man called as he hurried in behind her.

She barely turned her head. "Go throw yourself off the battlements for all I care, Siphuncle." She strode on toward Lady Maudelaine, who held her ground but groped behind her with one hand on the table. "Before I throw you off myself," Svarabakti added in a postscript to Siphuncle, stopping him in mid stride.

"You—she bore down on Lady Maudelaine—"you think *you* can humiliate me? I'll show you the meaning of the word. You wished to make a conquest of both Siphuncle, my discarded lover, and poor Roderick, your host? You wished to be admired in this gathering of celebrities in which you should never have normally dared show your face? Where *will* you show your face, you bleached and brazen brat, once I've properly knocked you cross-eyed?"

Svarabakti raised a hand armed with formidable nails lacquered a dark garnet red and further armed with a set of rings knobbed and spiked with jewels of considerable size.

Siphuncle leaped forward and caught the furious woman by the shoulders, trying to drag her backward.

But not before Svarabakti swung her palm in a thunderclap against the side of Maudelaine's face and dragged her hand away, leaving four red seeping nail cuts.

At the sight of blood, the crowd of onlookers became galvanized by instinctive impulses, some to scream, some to faint, some to flee, some to strive to drag the two women apart.

Garamond and Kennes stood their ground—Kennes because Venga Avests don't become embroiled in such squabbles; Garamond because it didn't seem Maudelaine would be too damaged to tell him about the parchment, and as far as he was concerned, the parchment held priority over a couple of jealous females.

He noted that the red-whiskered Shardé reacted only to hold his calligraphy brush, ink pouch, and his Do Not Disturb sign—neatly rolled—out of harm's way in the prehensile tip of his tail. The tail tip, knobbed along the lower side with two neat lines of black nubs, rather like the false feet of a caterpillar, was excellently designed for such work, and acted as a personal footman, ready to take over any menial tasks while the front half of a Shardé was better occupied.

To the onlookers it was only a squabble from which they would return their attention to the remnants of breakfast once they had suitably indulged their emotions.

Until they saw the knife.

The image seemed isolated and of unreal duration, like a glimpse seen by lightning flare between dark and dark.

Siphuncle hauled at Svarabakti's shoulders, dragging her backward. The fabric of her floating garnet gown bunched in his hands and drew up, tightening painfully across her throat.

Svarabakti twisted to free herself and raised and crossed her arms to wrench and scratch at Siphuncle's hands.

At a discreet signal from Borcubast, two Kulmar footmen with impassive faces stepped forward to take Maudelaine by the arms.

Before they touched her, she brought up the hand with which she had felt along the buffet table behind her. She held a wide, gleaming blade intended for filleting bristlefish. The hilt was jeweled, the blade ornate, engraved in a pattern of two bristlefish dodging the coils of a surf serpent. Yet it was deadly sharp.

For an incalculable moment, there might have been nothing in all that room but the pale hand tight around the elaborate hilt.

Garamond stuffed the rest of his sweet muffin into his mouth, shook out the lace napkin and tucked it, like a neckerchief, over the clasp of his cloak, adding the final panache that had been missing from his garb. He put a hand to his blaster and felt its comforting weight and balance. He hadn't the slightest idea what he expected to do with it.

Lady Maudelaine, the scarlet gashes showing vividly on her pallor, raised the knife until it almost touched her rival's nose. "Would you like to try that again?" she asked with false sweetness. She then lowered the blade and allowed the footmen to escort her away.

15

Conversation in the breakfast room gradually returned to normal. Those who had fainted were revived with jaffa and tender caresses; those who screamed were stifled with cream buns, a good shaking, and, in a few unfortunate cases, jugs of ice water applied externally.

Garamond had no desire to be noticed by Kennes so he slipped quietly away to begin an exploration of his own. He started down the first cross corridor he came to, trying doors as he went. A number of them were locked, and he wondered if he would soon have the assistance of his lock expert cousin.

Or ever.

He felt comforted to have heard that Lord Roderick had been sufficiently injured to stay out of the way. If Usher were indeed in a coma, he would not be able to answer vital questions about his intentions in obtaining the parchment. On the other hand, in a coma, he wouldn't be able to ask any embarrassing questions himself.

Such as why an uninvited guest was trying all the doors he could find.

Linen room. Gun room. Study—a brown study, what else? Cloakroom. Malachite morning room—a chill room, where green stone gryphons with half-raised wings looked down from picturesque pedestals. Writing room, with a collection of Elbe-Esque inkpots, and a door giving onto...a display of Shardé calligraphy.

Calligraphy! Walls and ceiling were papered with purple parchment written over in ornate gold in what might be a rude joke played by Usher upon his investigators. Would he actually hide a purple parchment in as appropriate a place as a room of purple parchments? A room not only papered with them, but with ornate cases displaying some individually, some bound into books encased in purple silk. Even the candle sconces, Garamond noted wryly, were gilded and hung with amethyst pendants.

With sudden shock, Garamond realized that he knew no way to recognize the missing parchment except by its color. A jolly lot of good that would do him now. He plunked into the middle of a purple couch with black tassles, head in hands.

He tried to think, shutting his eyes against a plethora of purples. Think? Thinking was Gwen's job.

Silly old Gwen, grubbing in some silly old niche when she should have simply come in through the front door. Then she'd be here among the parchments. Helping him think.

A purple parchment, written in gold, about that big, Kennes had said. Written by the Shardé Native Chief, it seemed, and with such a sensitive message that Usher could blackmail the chief and the governor with it.

Garamond might not be so good in the logic department, but he could jolly well read.

He started just to the right of the door by which he had entered, stood on a convenient chair, and began with the topmost scroll.

"Whereas, by his munificent efforts on behalf of the Shardé Native Ladies Historical Society and Jaffa Club, We the undersigned elevate Lord Roderick Usher to Honorary. . .

"Whereas Lord Roderick Usher has donated a complete one-hundred-place set of Rumpleworth yellow-on-green ceramic dinnerware (Th'ing Dynasty) to the Shardé Native Chief's Simple Woodland Palace . . .

"Whereas Imperial Ambassador Lord Roderick Usher so ably served the People of Shard in their Time of Trouble by donating a Memorial Fountain for those slain in the Shardé Separatist Uprising . . ."

Garamond had just stepped down to move the chair over to the next row of documents when a strangled voice, outside and above, screamed, "Murder!"

He leaped to the window and found that it led to a balcony. From the balcony he heard another throttled scream high above him, but looking up saw nothing except the mass of the ancient fortress climbing against the sky.

From the balcony a stairway led diagonally around the outer wall of the turret that housed the parchment room. Here and there the stair's balustrades had crumbled away, now falling sheer onto rocks three or four floors below, now vanishing into the depths of the tarn.

Without hesitation, Garamond ran up the stairway. Where he

finally stopped for breath, heavy-footed, the stairway stopped too. Only a narrow arch soared across the gulf between this tower and the next.

After a brief pause, Garamond bounded across, trying for once not to step too heavily.

At the other end he ascended a spiral stair that encircled the tower to its summit, a circular flagstoned space with a clear view over the tarn, but with the bulk of the mansion still clawing at the clouds on the other side.

Lightheaded from his charge, Garamond rested his elbows on the parapet. Leaning outward, he could see the emerald lawn where the revelers once more practiced their capers. Wafts of music drifted up to him with the heavy, sulphurous airs off the water below. Beyond the tarn, swells of moorland stretched away, toothed with gray stone. Garamond traced the sinuous pewter line of slow water that fed the tarn and slipped reluctantly away over a shelf of rotting stone to emerge in unexpected gleams beyond the hills.

He saw the minute fluorescent mark of the portation hatch nearly at the horizon, and from it, the four paths of the crossroads, gossamer lines in the distance. Here and there the moorland heights sheltered a farm. On one, Garamond saw the miniature forms of distant Shardé gleaning rows of reddish grain. He started violently at the nearby cry, "Murder! Mur-der!"

Garamond leaned over the parapet, drawing his blaster. A sudden gust of wind nearly toppled him, and as he recovered, a scuffle of wings beat over him and a large male pootock in full autumnal plumage landed neatly on his blaster barrel.

The pheasantlike russet bird shuffled its graduated fringed scales. The longest of these formed tawny flight feathers and an ebony tail of ribbonlike plumes. It tilted its wide, guileless face and winked coyly. "Murder?" it asked ingratiatingly.

This wasn't the first time Garamond had been fooled by the cry of a pootock in the grounds of a stately house. The feckless bird, with a body about the size of Garamond's head, was amazingly light on his blaster, and undeniably decorative, if overly loud and misleading in its cry. He transferred the creature to his left wrist and holstered his weapon. He felt particularly exposed on the tower top, and looked up at the higher towers for sentries watching him.

The only sentry he could discover seemed to be paying attention only to the contents of his grog skin. Yet Garamond could have sworn someone was watching him, even as he watched for watchers.

The trapdoor onto the platform creaked open menacingly, making the pootock flutter hastily onto his shoulder. "Euh, young master, have ye got a pootuck?" asked an aged Kulmar who Garamond recognized with relief as the butler. With less relief he remembered that in the universal history of butlers, these retainers could be divided into two subsets: perfect butlers and the butlers that dunnit.

"Here, chappie; here, chap. Come to Borcubast now." The butler fished vigorously in his pouch and produced a twist of candied rind in silver paper.

Overwhelmed with cupboard love, the pootock fluttered onto the old man's wrist, gulped the rind, and sat with its head stretched upward and its eyes closed in evident ecstasy as the comfit descended its gullet. Finally it bent and preened the glistening plumage over the spot where the tidbit had come to rest, and glanced up hopefully. "Help? Murder?" it asked.

"No more, old chap," Borcubast shook his head.

"Murder!" replied the disgruntled creature, and flew off.

"I say, Borcubast, this is rather an edifice, what?" Garamond felt quite pleased at having divined the butler's name, unaware that the canny retainer had introduced it for that very purpose.

"'Tis generally fancied to be quite an edifice, sir." The butler hesitated to say "m'lord." The guest he faced possessed a self-satisfaction and mild vacancy often to be found among the aristocracy but lacked a certain benign expectation of all things to center around him. Nor had he the conscious intent to hold center stage, and thus could not be an actor, unless he was among the least or the greatest, and could yield it gracefully. "In fact, 'tis fancied to have a mind of its own, this house. Sentient, the master calls it. Leads people on, gets them lost, drops things on them. Very clever, for a house. 'Tis a mercy that there bridge didn't give way under ye, that bein' the low humour of this place."

"A fascinating house though, and I daresay I know a trick or two worth any it could play me. I'd like to be shown around some of the more noteworthy sights if anyone can be spared to guide me. Roderick knows my interest in ancient structures." With considerable embarrassment Garamond paused and asked, "He's all right, isn't he? Not at death's door or anything?"

"Not at all, not a bit of it. A bit fevered and out of temper, if you'll pardon my speakin' over-frank, but not never in no danger."

Garamond, at first glad to find that the butler hadn't asked him who he was and what he was doing up on this lonely tower, began to wonder if Borcubast might be up here for no good, in no position to ask questions himself.

"In fact, when I left his lordship," the butler elaborated, "he was a-sittin' by the window a-watchin' the practicin' for the revelments. Ye can hear 'em yet when the wind's right. To be tellin' more truth than 'tis my place, I didn't want to loiter around where he could send for me, lest in his pique he might ask me to throttle the most racketsome hornpiper, or put that freckle-faced, bagpipe strangling, womanizing fop—Kelesophos—in the dungeon.

"He's not a friend of yers, I hope," Borcubast inquired belatedly, "because if he is, ye've probably said worse of him yerself, but it's not my place to do it. But speaking of dungeons," he added with relief when Garamond withheld any wrath he may have felt on the part of the dudelsacker, "I'd be glad to show ye around here and there until I'm needed back in the buttery."

Borcubast lived to regret the offer.

16

Gwen, perched in her niche, looked through a bringle thicket to see a man approaching, hat at jaunty angle, signalling to unknown reinforcements under cover. At least he wasn't a sentry.

From long experience, Gwen knew sentries were nearly impossible people with whom to reason. Which is why they so often were replaced by unthinking systems.

The hidden camera, the sensor-laden lock, the security system that interfaced with an identification system—all were as vigilant, loyal, unbending, and gullible as live sentries.

Still, the odd busybody amateur could be a serious danger. Could stumble on the truth, or, just as easily stumble onto a false conclusion. Could shoot first and remember the consequences later.

The fellow who had interrupted Gwen's work looked as earnest and as amateur as she could imagine. He might as well be a toddler playing at some traditional game like Industrial Espionage or Peace Troops and Pirates. Whoever his reinforcements were, they were likely as infected as he with the fever of sleuth-for-a-day. The fellow had something under his cloak that might be a weapon, guaranteed to go off when least convenient.

Gwen suddenly would have preferred a platoon of Kulmar sentries, fully armed and armoured. At least they weren't apt to have inconvenient accidents with weaponry.

"What do you think you're doing up there?"

Gwen sat, apparently relaxed, on the lip of the niche. Her blaster lay beside her in full view, and she kept her hands away from it by a good distance.

What did she think she was doing up there?

"Actually, I was thinking of planting a medium charge explosive to blow away this end of the house and expose the subterranean treasuries." She waited for the sarcasm to sink in. She could count the seconds. Six, seven . . .

"Ha! Jolly good joke, that. Subterranean treasuries. I'll have to tell poor old Roddy that one if he ever recovers."

"Ever recovers?" Gwen asked with sharp concern. "What's happened to him?" For a moment she was all too sure that Garamond had done something foolish.

"Didn't you hear? Someone ponged him on the cranial dome. He's out of his mind with the fever, and they're afraid he'll never be the same." The young fellow looked blithely unconcerned. After all, he felt fine, and as long as he got his three meals and high tea, and a vast manor house to frolic in with good company, the fate of his host—this side of inconvenient death—meant little.

"Mercy." Gwen became all wide-eyed interest, though with continuing concern that Garamond had given Usher an ill-considered pong. "I haven't heard a thing about it. I stayed out here all the night," (after all, her visitor might stumble upon signs of their encampment) "so as to get down to my investigation as soon as possible after dawn.

"You have to realize," she elaborated, "that I make rather a hobby of antique archirtecture. Our host had been somewhat concerned that the major stress-carrying buttressed bastions at the west end here had begun to deteriorate. I told him I'd take it as a special favor if he let me poke about a bit and take some readings of the architectonic structural stresses before he brought in professionals. I'm glad to say that other than this niche, which needs to be recemented, everything is perfectly sound."

Considerably daunted by the terminology, the young man backed away as if expecting the entire west wing to collapse at any moment, and tripped sprawling over Gwen's pack.

"Oh, I say, terribly sorry, miss. Would you like me to hand it up to you?"

Gwen, fearful of expressing concern at the thought of a stranger handling her personal set of burglarous devices, merely smiled tightly.

"Oh, I say, I seem to be holding it upside down," the young chap muttered with mild embarrassment as the contents cascaded from the pack.

Gwen wondered if *she* could use that innocent-seeming technique to search people's belongings under their noses.

"Oh, I say, you aren't a Fausta agent, miss?" The young man blushed around a goodly crop of rich freckles. It was a blush of excitement. Gwen could almost hear him inventing press releases:

Youthful Amateur Detective Single-handedly Captures Fausta
Ring at Imperial Ambassador's Mansion. The youthful detective,
blissfully ignoring explosives, night-vision scopes, tri-vi cameras
cunningly disguised as pocketknives and pocketknives cunningly
disguised as toothpick cases, unerringly held up the piece of webwire, the most damning and most innocent item from the pack.

"Stars and rockets, miss, then the Fausta really are funding the
Shardé Separatist Movement."

It was the first Gwen had heard of it, and she said so. Several
times. Disclaiming any membership in the Fausta.

She only succeeded in confusing the young fellow badly. She
saw that he had a tighter grip on whatever he held under his
cloak. A confused armed person is almost as dangerous as a
frightened one. Gwen spoke very slowly and very firmly.

I'm Gwen Gray. I'm not a Fausta member, but someone at this
house is, if this wire means anything. I simply found it on the
ground. At first I thought it might be a trip-trap, but it wasn't. I
merely put it in my pack to check on later. After I checked the
structural cohesion of the west wing.

"Now, there's only one of me, and I only have one blaster.
I've been using it for structural soundings and stress readings. I'm
going to leave it where it is and come down and sit on the end of
these steps.

"You call up whoever came with you, and we'll all have a
council meeting. Something very odd is going on, and we have to
figure it out. You know how important something like a Fausta
plot would be to an Imperial Ambassador."

The young man tried to look as if he understood, and whistled
up his henchmen, a girl named Patrice and a Shardé named
Hyota-ya. The young man was called Kelosophos and, as it
turned out, carried nothing more dangerous than a dudelsack. Not
that it didn't make awfully pungent music.

"All right," Gwen began, trying to keep the discussion at a
level her audience could appreciate, "in a few days, Shard will
become a Commonwealth of the Empire. But because you discovered a piece of Fausta webwire here on Shard, we know that the
Empire is in danger and only fast work on your parts can save it.
How do you know about the Fausta funding a Separatist movement?"

Patrice spoke up brightly. "From Yotu. He's an artist and a
Separatist ringleader and he doesn't care who knows. He's always
saying silly things about Imperial overlords, but we always

thought that was just talk. He was saying a lot of things about the Fausta Freedom Fighters the other night at dinner, but I don't think many people were listening."

"Because the governor's daughter had just come," Kelesophos explained, "and everyone was watching her try to get Siphuncle away from Svarabakti." He plucked a young sedge frond and began to chew on the white inner end of it.

"But I'm *not* a Separatist. I don't think it's a lasting fashion— even as a schism." Hyota-ya took the webwire and played three-handed cat's cradle with the aid of his tail.

"Oh, I say, Kelesophos, you *were* right. Borcubast can't have blipped Usher on the noggin. I remember something about him finding a bit of webwire where the arch collapsed on Roderick, or whatever it was that laid him in his bed of pain. It *must* have been a Fausta trip-trap.

"But the Separatists," Hyota-ya continued, "should have given it up as a bad idea after the uprising—once you saw people dead in the dust, you could see it wasn't a stylish revolution. Compared to our old Vonyushar overlords, the Oriel-Mossmarching Empire is so wondrously aesthetic—except perhaps the Empress's taste in hats—that I see no reason to resist."

Hyota-ya held up a wire web as complex as lacework, made a few adjustments to it, and continued:

"I'm a proper Loyalist and I know that the greatest danger to the Empire is Separatism. We have the vastest and most powerful Empire in the history of known space, and we have never contacted another political or social entity we couldn't absorb. We Shardé are an example. But any unit that tries to break away from the Empire is a weak link in the bureaucratic chain."

Gwen felt incredulous amazement at the number of Imperial textbook clichés the Shardé had compressed into one speech. "That's why," she explained, "the Empire is making Shard part of the Imperial Commonwealth instead of a colony. It satisfies both the Loyalists and the Separatists to just the point of equilibrium."

Patrice tucked a curl into place and frowned becomingly at Kelesophos. "But the Fausta are independent privateers, and they haven't destroyed the Empire," she said.

"That," Kelesophos explained around his sedge frond, "is because they aren't really a large organization. Every little band of marauders flies the Triple Serpent banner and claims the backing of the Fausta, but it's all little bands that can't really unite in a show of force. I saw a thing about it on vid."

"Then why," Gwen asked with considerable interest, "would the local Fausta branch back the local Separatist branch? Without a close link to the Empire, Shard would lose the sort of trade the Fausta thrives on."

Hyota-ya allowed his tail to take over the webwire, leaving both hands free for expansive gestures. "Yotu says that if there was another Separatist uprising, the Empress would send out the navy." He licked the end of his nose and whuffled earnestly.

Gwen nodded.

"But probably only one or two light cruisers because, truth to tell, we Shardé are an easygoing sort, and don't find uprisings particularly stylish."

The noticably fashion-conscious Patrice appeared to file this valuable information.

"And"—Hyota-ya paused for dramatic effect—"the local Fausta would adore capturing a navy cruiser."

It was clear to Gwen that matters could become far worse than Perugius, Kennes, or the governor had suggested. She almost felt that it was up to her to save the Empire—or at least a couple of its cruisers—with little help but that of a freckle-faced bagpiper, a clotheshorse, and a long-tailed loyalist.

If only Garamond had stayed around to listen to this, he'd be in a position to take action. What action, she wasn't very sure, but she could always count on Garamond to take action.

She hurriedly sent her intelligence team, such as it was, back around to the practicing revelers to do some creative listening. She could think things through a good deal better without their earnestly sophomoric company.

She returned to the niche and loosened a particularly large and crucial stone.

Only then did she realize that in the company of Kelesophos and friends she could have entered the manor house by the front door with no trouble whatsoever.

17

Tours of imposing edifices all have a lot in common. The visitor is sorely tested in his ability to climb stairs and plod down limitless corridors, to absorb names, dates, and other such facts, and to appear interested. The visitor only knows, unless his guide is the owner of the edifice, that his guide, too, would just as soon sit down halfway through the tour, remove his shoes, and have a cold drink. Humanity is limited in its vicarious pleasure at another's possessions.

Borcubast's bent old shanks carried him down echoing halls and twisting, labyrinthine stairs. Following the butler's bald pate like a beacon light, Garamond paced studiously behind.

"These here pilasters are all red marble from his lordship's quarries in the Calcimine Uplands. Many a time I've heered him say as no better beetsblood red ever came out o' the Uplands."

"Ah," said Garamond. "Semisomewhat neobaroque," he added.

"This here portrait of his lordship were painted by Comrey Bhevlic durin' his Lucid Period." A not particularly lucid Lord Roderick stared feverishly from the frame.

"A good likeness," said Garamond. "Bhevlic's last lucidity, I fancy."

"These here vases from the Ashpit Th'ing dynasty was given to his lordship by the Empress herself in appreciation . . ."

Pseudo-Th'ing, aged in kitchen compost, Garamond corrected silently.

". . . of his aid in a time of crisis. Financial crisis, I understand, that being the kind his lordship is most fit to deal with."

"Ah," said Garamond.

"See this painted panel here, sir, with the chappie drawn to look like his lordship a-weeping over a lady's tombstone? Well, if ye press here on this carved cherrybim in the frame, like, the whole thing—watch out—swings back, and there's the secret passage to the Sunset Chapel where his lordship has memorials to all his sainted ancestors, with a great gold angel a-watching over his mother so as to touch yer heart."

After enduring the chappie weeping on the tombstone, Garamond hardly thought he could face a sorrowing angel, gold or otherwise, but he had a professional interest in secret passages, and followed uncomplaining.

Stairs descended at a breakneck angle in utter darkness, leading to chambers and passages whose dimensions could only be guessed by the quality of echoes they gave back. A scent of seepage from springs below the tarn added to the atmosphere of melancholy. Garamond, who always preferred a certain amount of light in his explorations, felt a degree of depression only Lord Roderick could have appreciated.

"His lordship finds this passage handy for nipping over to the chapel unnoticed when he's a bit downhearted-like."

"Ah," said Garamond, and tried not to voice the groan he felt. Something was surely watching him down in the dark. The whole house, imbued with secret malice, must be watching him, waiting . . .

"And ye come out here through this little vestry . . ."

They climbed a narrow stairway and emerged, after a frustrating scuffle with the door latch, into the dim light of chapel candles.

Garamond, though he normally had the perfunctory sort of religion of convenience common to his generation, could have knelt and thanked numerous celestial beings, hypothetical or otherwise, for the blessing of light after the claustrophobic passage behind him.

He looked around for a more traditional entrance and found, with enormous relief, an ornate arched doorway opening out into an ostentatiously onyx paneled hall, with torches in every sconce. Only then could Garamond return his attention to the chapel. High-arched ceiling, semicircular niches along the walls, statuary of the flamboyant type more forgivable in halls of prayer than in halls of pleasure, though similar in design—it was a chapel quite in keeping with the rest of the structure. Garamond wondered if it had served as a chapel back in the time this had been a Vonyushar fortress. Perhaps the Vonyushar had laid the fruits of their military victories on the high altar.

Rather odd sculpture on the altar now, come to think of it. Must be one of Lord Roderick's personal touches. What saint would be carved to lie on the altar, her gown the colour of blood on the white and gold of the altar cloth?

Where everything else reflected orthodox High Church Rickchucktarianism with the twin martyred prophets lovingly portrayed in Gothic splendor of porphyry and gold, the saint on the altar smacked of heresy—not out of character for Lord Roderick.

Not Saint Mabel, patron of hyperspace travel.

Not Saint Claudine, to whom all beings were brothers, no matter the number of their eyes or tentacles.

Not Saint Svarabakti. No saint she.

But Svarabakti lay upon the altar, in gown of garnet red, echoed by the brilliant cut garnets clasped around her throat. What an odd religious affectation, to lie at length on one's host's altar. As if one were an object of worship. As if one were the dead carved on a tomb.

Dead.

Of course she was dead.

The living don't wear ornate fish knives plunged between their breasts.

Where was that dratted butler? Ah, over lighting a candle, muttering something about his "master's recovery." Completely oblivious to what lay where it so obviously shouldn't.

Garamond felt a sudden concern for the bent old man. How much of a shock could he stand?

"I say, Borcubast, old fellow, I seem to have a spot of bad news."

The old butler turned toward him slowly, his eyes unreadable. "If ye mean that she-witch on the altar," he said with growing heat, "it may be news, but I can't say it's bad. A nastier bloodsucking besom I hope never to see, and if she's gone and bebloodied that there hand-embroidered Khaarn-work altar cloth, I hope her soul haunts the underpits, I do."

18

$\mathbf{G}$aramond and the butler approached the altar with a certain reverence both for the place and for the dead. Not for the person she had been, but for the fact of death.

"You don't think she did this to herself, Borcubast?" Garamond had no hope that the matter would be that simple.

" 'Twasn't a mannerly way to go, and she weren't mannerly." Borcubast scuffed a few steps closer over the marble floor. He frowned into the wide, brown, unseeing eyes. "If she's done herself in, she's saved a mighty lot of people the trouble."

Garamond began to realize how complicated it would be to have a corpse in this isolated house. Presumably, one could call from the house and give the authorities the portal coordinates. If Roderick Usher wished. If he didn't wish, one could walk back to the portal, portage to Kettlewharf, send in authorities on one's own coded token.... Unless the Peace Office had the Usher house coordinates, and Garamond felt rather afraid they didn't. Would the Peace Troops of Kettlewharf then have to fight their way in against Usher's Kulmar sentries?

He turned to the butler. "The last I knew, most of the guests were out practicing the Commonwealth Day revelry. Go down, quick as you can, and lock the front door. And any other doors you know of." Under the circumstances, he was willing to admit he might have missed an entrance.

"There ain't none other. Just windows. This used to be a fortyfication, ye know." Borcubast was already halfway down the chapel aisle, speaking over his shoulder.

"Then make a list of everyone who's inside and everyone who's outside, and then tell Lord Roderick. I'll wait here."

He waited.

He realized after a while that he didn't know his way back in any case. He wouldn't try the subterranean passages without a

torch, not for any reason. He could probably find his way back
through the ornate arched doorway, but it would take a good
while. He wasn't in any hurry.

Svarabakti was in no hurry at all.

Her hand was still warm and limp, like the sister's in that story
that had coloured all Roderick Usher's life. But she wasn't going
to waken and claw her way out of her tomb.

Not with a fish knife in her.

They must have come the whole length of the house, Garamond and Borcubast and Svarabakti and her murderer. The
manor door faced the sunrise, and this was called the Sunset
Chapel.

Garamond was watching the corpse, and he felt certain someone was watching him.

All the chapel shone silver and gold and red and black. As
if in some fateful heraldry, the corpse bore the same colors. He
remembered an old story-tale of an evil queen with face white
as foam, hair black as night, and lips red as blood. This might
have been she, in a garnet gown edged in gold, in a chapel of
golden saints and onyx columns and a floor of red and white
marble squares, as always in a chapel of the Rickchucktarians.
Red for Saint Richard and white for Saint Charles. Or perhaps
it was the other way around. All Garamond knew was that it
had been a terrible heresy to have it the wrong way—with a
white square where a red should be—and a holy war had been
fought long ago, but the heretics had never been defeated, and
even today there were secret sects of Rickchucktarians meeting
in hidden places with the floors tiled the other way.

Someone was surely watching him. A shadow fluttered behind
a still saint in his niche.

"Have you realized there's not jolly much blood for a stab-
bing, Gar?"

Now that he considered it, there wasn't all that much blood.

And now that he thought of it, at the back of some of the
chapel niches there were windows, and one of them might have
been sealed up long ago. But not sealed well enough. Gwen had
been right after all. About that, anyhow.

Now she and Garamond looked at the dead woman. Svarabakti's garnet-colored gown concealed the flow of blood at first
glance. When one looked closer, a discolouration could be seen

and a sticking of the gauze fabric to the body around the knife hilt. Not very far around it, though.

Gwen, with notable detachment, pointed out, "I don't know who she is or why she's here, but she certainly wasn't killed with that knife."

19

Garamond had gotten to the interesting parts of a description of the altercations in the breakfast room when a man's voice from the ornate archway pronounced, "The form of human sacrifice I see before me is hardly consistent with orthodox Rickchucktarianism."

Gwen and Garamond swung around to confront Gaust Kennes. Or perhaps the Venga Avest of Corbo. In any event, he had made his pronouncement with a straight face.

Gwen sat on the carved arm of a pew, exposing the full extent of one kneecap. "Are you a specialist in the forms of human sacrifice? Are such practices likely in this household?"

"It is hardly for a Venga Avest to pronounce on so unfashionable a practice as ritual murder. My apologies, Miss Gray, Mr. Gray, I should have greeted you sooner, but I find this desecration so shocking, I momentarily forgot myself."

Gwen stared.

Garamond muttered, unfortunately loud enough for the chapel's acoustics to carry admirably, "He's being the Venga Avest of Corbo."

Gwen forgot that she was a sophisticated woman of the worlds. "What's a Venga Avest? I've never heard of one," she admitted frankly. It was something no one else in the Usher manor had yet asked. The Grays, who knew Kennes as the governor's agent, waited in considerable suspense for the answer.

With difficulty, Kennes drew his attention away from the remarkable corpse. "Actually, I must admit that the title of Venga Avest is a transcendent one, which applies to me on a different plane than that in which my corporeal body resides."

Kennes made a noticeable effort to sound like himself. He was not particularly successful. "Actually, I made it up. It has often been considered . . ." he began again in the dignified tones of the Venga Avest, realized how he sounded, and admitted sheepishly, "Now that I've been playing a Venga Avest since yesterday evening, it's hard to get out of the role. It's rather alarming, but I like being a Venga Avest, and if I may say so, I think I'm a rather good one.

"But"—and his gaze returned with undiminished fascination to Svarabakti's corpse on the altar—"Lord Roderick seems to have a death on his hands."

The Grays maintained a thoughtful silence.

"I don't mean," Kennes elaborated, "that I think Roderick did this terrible thing." He looked the Grays over as if with consideration of the possibility that they had thought so. "I mean only that tragedy has touched his house. I met the old butler as I was contemplating an odd painting in the great hall, the one of our host by Comrey Bhevlic during his Lucid Period—Bhevlic's—and the old fellow, the butler, looked rather shaken, so I asked him if anything else was amiss, and he admitted that I might be a spiritual comfort to a poor, departed soul."

Kennes paused.

"When did you see her last?" Garamond questioned him, just as Gwen asked, "Did you see her after breakfast?" and Kennes queried, "When did you last encounter the unfortunate Svarabakti?"

Somehow all the sentences became untangled, but no one admitted to having seen the woman from the time Siphuncle had led her away from the breakfast room to the time Garamond and Borcubast had discovered the death.

"Where have you been in the meantime?" Gwen asked hurriedly, afraid Kennes would ask simultaneously.

Apparently Garamond and Kennes had both been exploring. They had, at different times, discovered several of the same places. However, since Kennes didn't mention finding a room of purple parchments, Garamond didn't mention it either. Gwen explained how and when she had entered the manor. She realized that it sounded unlikely and coincidental that she should arrive where, and all too close to when, the body had been discovered. Kennes didn't comment on how peculiar this seemed.

Kennes finally asked, "Do you think this has anything to do with the other . . . business?"

The three came to the consensus that it didn't seem likely, but it wasn't impossible.

As they talked, Svarabakti lay in decorative death, with no effect whatsoever on their composure. No noticeable effect. Gwen mentioned this.

"Perhaps," Garamond suggested, "it's because she doesn't look dead. Or even real. Like one more sculptured saint. That's what I thought at first. Not that she was any saint at breakfast," he added.

"It's like a theatrical tableau," Kennes elaborated. He still looked at the body with a calm fascination. Apparently calm. The Grays couldn't imagine his thoughts. "It's an operatic pose. Vaster and more vivid than ordinary life." Opera had recently become enormously popular in the Empire, or at least in those parts of the Empire where it mattered what was considered fashionable. Such as Shard.

"It's an aesthetic corpse." Kennes, still watching the dead woman, seemed unable to stop referring to her, as if he were done speaking but could not be done with the subject. "Not like the corpses . . . in combat."

The Grays' files on Kennes had given them no reason to believe he had seen combat, but they waited silently.

"I saw a bit of the Shardé Separatist Uprising." Kennes seemed reluctant to speak, reluctant to stop speaking. The look of the corpse, or the fact of the corpse, seemed to hold him mesmerized. "A body"—he hesitated—"human or Shardé, looks rather different in the dust of the street, after blaster fire. Or bobbing in a fountain." Perhaps the indignity of the thought of a dead person floating in one of Kettlewharf's many ostentatious fountains made him begin to laugh.

He couldn't stop himself, and the sound seemed more shocking and insane than the sight of a woman coolly sleeping her last sleep.

Garamond stepped aside and flipped the edge of the altar cloth over Svarabakti's face. With another corner of the stiffly embroidered cloth, he covered the hilt of the knife. An eloquent outline remained beneath the fabric, but the effect had changed.

Gwen stood and put one hand on each side of Kennes' face. She held him by the ears, not so as to give pain, but as if he had been a recalcitrant child to whom something must be made clear. She said, "Nothing is all right, and you're not going to be just fine."

Kennes wondered if anyone had ever before told such truth in a crisis, and the shock of it was such that he got his breath back. "No one takes the Venga Avest by the ears," he intoned, and withdrew from Gwen's grip.

This, understandably, did not convince her that he had all his wits about him, but he seemed further from hysterics.

The three walked out into the adjoining ostentatious onyx hall and sat on an ornate onyx bench in a niche designed to display a vast black glass sculpture of a mourning naiad.

Here they discussed practical matters. They could not conclude who had killed Svarabakti, or how, but they reminded one another of Lady Maudelaine's behavior at breakfast. They agreed that they had no reason to tell anyone that any of the three were investigators, but the unspoken thought hung heavy that Kennes had no reason to trust the Grays, nor they he. However, he was the governor's agent, and as such might know a thing or two worth knowing. Gwen asked him if he knew anything about the Fausta funding the Shardé Separatist Movement.

This was the first Garamond had heard of the matter, and he had to have it explained in detail before he would yield the floor to Kennes. By that time Kennes had heard everything Gwen knew, so she had some doubts that his information had the freshness and spontaneity it would have had if Garamond had not interrupted.

Kennes pondered. It was, he said, the kind of thing that Separatists and Fausta members avoided saying too close to the governor or his agent. If they had, something would have been done about it.

Garamond and Gwen avoided looking at one another. All too often high officials had accepted much-needed funding of essential programs in return for not looking into certain matters. It would be an interesting way, for example, to obtain a new Goff copse. *Then,* Gwen thought, her imagination taking the bit in its teeth, *when the Fausta tried to capture the naval vessel after the hypothetical second Separatist uprising, the governor and his agent, if they were involved, could put up a noticeable, if ineffective, show of Loyalist force. After which they could retire with decorations from a grateful, if ignorant, Empire, and play Goff.*

"Still"—Kennes furrowed his brow, fortunately unaware of the treason he had committed in Gwen's mind—"I seem to recall . . . Yes. When Usher called the governor's mansion about having the significant document, I believe he said something about thinking it might be equally valuable to the Fausta."

20

In time, the onyx room became melancholy of itself. At first the Grays and Kennes thought that they had become unexpectedly depressed by the presence in the chapel of the dead. "I daresay we're just tired," Gwen hazarded. "After all, it must be long past lunchtime. Once we've eaten, we'll probably feel better."

This didn't seem likely. The three looked at their futures as gray and shadowy lands stretching featureless to far and unwelcome horizons. "Perhaps it's the house," Garamond suggested. "The butler mentioned that the house has a life of its own. That it's sentient." This too seemed unlikely, but the room appeared to mourn, and the black glass sea-maid in her niche seemed past weeping.

Footfalls echoed. Boots rang and half armour jingled. Behind them came the flap of soft shoes.

The butler had brought an honour guard of Kulmar sentries for the dead. Two carried a high, narrow, black banner on gilded spears. Two carried a vaster banner, black velvet fringed with black, on pikes topped with black plumes. At Borcubast's instruction, they entered the chapel.

Garamond, weighted down with melancholy, found it an effort to rise. He rose, nevertheless, and protested. One did not move or touch corpses until the Peace Office had a look at them. Still, in this house, the Peace Office at Kettlewharf seemed as far away as the Imperial Court, half a galaxy away. The butler explained with great patience and dignity that Lord Roderick had ordered that the body be placed in the room appointed for such things, to lie in state until it could be entombed in the subterranean catacombs.

At the thought of the subterranean catacombs, Garamond subsided. Resignedly he waved the honour guard into the chapel.

In due time, walking solemnly and slowly, they reappeared, carrying the body on the narrow banner, all but the face covered over by the drape of velvet. They placed it on an onyx table in the onyx room, and the black glass naiad sorrowed over her. The sense of melancholy pervading the room increased to a sense of vast tragedy. The room seemed well satisfied with its role.

The four Kulmar sentries, two pairs of identical twins, each stood at a corner of the table they had made into a bier. They wore traditional, if impractical, half armour of dark leather vests, armbands, and caplike helms, all sheathed in ornamented bronze scales. These, worn with scarlet-fringed black breechcloths and bronze-studded fighting sandals accentuated tanned limbs and heads of startlingly blond hair hanging straight to their massive shoulders.

Following Borcubast, the Grays and Kennes (once more the Venga Avest of Corbo) discovered most of the rest of the party taking tea in a room hung with pale gold brocade. Footmen served jaffa, and actual tea for those who cared for it, with water leaf sandwiches and three kinds of cake. Kennes opted to stay and listen, which pleased the Grays, who didn't care to have him listen to them—unless he could be proven innocent. He seemed to feel similarly about them.

At Garamond's suggestion, Borcubast signalled to a footman, who set about loading a large tray with delicacies. The butler led the Grays up a maze of stairways and hallways to Lord Roderick's room, followed at a respectful distance by the heavily laden footman.

Lord Roderick reclined on tapestry cushions piled onto a couch near a narrow mullioned window. His pale face and large liquid eyes showed the ravages of fever, and his dark hair of gossamer fineness contrasted harshly with the white bandage with which it was bound, and the other that formed a sling for his arm.

Wearing his pomegranate-colored velvet robe edged with black watered silk, he appeared at one with the overexquisite furnishings in the same color scheme.

"Yer Lordship," his butler addressed him, trying to judge whether Usher remembered the names of these guests, "it were Garamond Gray, here, as discovered Miss Svarabakti's body, and his, er, cousin Gwen Gray who joined him, with His Excellency, the Venga Avest of Corbo, in a-watching over the corpus until I could get some sentries into the mourning room." Both Borcubast and Lord Roderick looked discreetly pleased to have avoided the presence of the Venga Avest.

Lord Roderick nodded the Grays into uncomfortably hard upholstered chairs that had been made to his Gothic specifications. "Garamond, Gwen"—he made brief nods as if his head pained him—"I deeply regret your having been inconvenienced by this unfortunate occurrence. For the sake of my other guests, I am glad to say that diplomatic immunity frees me of the need to call in the Kettlewharf Peace Troops. The presence of troopers at our gathering could only add insult to the injury of our having lost one of our number."

Usher, realizing from the Grays' silence that he should make some acknowledgment of convention, added, "Don't think, because I will not harbour the local Peace Troops, that I condone violence done in my house. However, like Monsieur C. August Dupin, my brother in literature, I have a certain detective ability, and when I have determined the culprit, I will inform the authorities, if circumstances warrant. You must understand that in the diplomatic world, circumstances must sometimes be interpreted differently than in ordinary life. Still, this resembles a momentary crime of passion."

A wicked smile touched his lips. "Unfortunately, due to the generous manner in which Svarabakti carried on her amours, the list of those possibly concerned is rather long."

Usher signalled the footman to set down his tray and depart. His master remembered rather late what a talkative footman Brennu was, and suspected that the kitchen staff would hear everything just mentioned. The footman, a remarkably good friend of one of the maids, closed the door deferentially behind him and listened for a moment.

Borcubast, speaking loudly enough for the footman (whom he suspected of hovering outside) to hear that he wasn't going to hear anything, began, "Yer Lordship?"

"Yes, Borcubast."

"Well, His Excellency the Venga Avest of Corbo should by rights have a better room than the Red Death Tappystry room. Hadn't I ought to put him in the Valdemar Suite?"

Usher nodded.

Borcubast turned to the Grays. "We put popes and imams and maharishis and lapidomantists and such-all clergy in the Valdemar. Also"—he turned back to Lord Roderick—"shouldn't I better make a note to return the garnets, as Miss Svarabakti was wearin', to Lady Maudelaine? Before the burial but after ye've investygated this an' that." Usher nodded again and put his hand to his forehead.

"I noticed," Gwen pointed out to Borcubast, "that one of the mortared-up windows at the back of a niche in the chapel has come open. It lets in a draught and who knows what else."

"I'll have it seen to." The butler bowed formally. "And speakin', as I was, of Yer Lordship's investygations, I made up a list of them as was outside and them as was inside at the time in question, for you to ask 'em as to odd occurrences, such as stabbings and all."

Garamond offered, "I saw an odd occurrence in the morning room."

"The mourning room?"

"Yes. Lady Maudelaine—"

"She has already heard of the sad event? I wouldn't have thought she would pay her respects so soon—or with any sincerity," Usher added.

"Oh, at the time I'm speaking of, Svarabakti was still alive. She came in to breakfast and threatened—"

"I see, the morning room. Of course."

"Yes, as I said, and threatened Lady Maudelaine, who returned the threat with a fish knife. The same, or one of the precise design, as that with which Svarabakti was stabbed.

Usher passed his good hand across his upper lip. "An impulsive young lady, Lady Maudelaine, but not a bad sort."

"In her . . . statement," Garamond volunteered, "Svarabakti implied that she and Siphuncle had had a love affair that came to a bad end, and that she saw Maudelaine as her rival. This suggests that she and Siphuncle might also have been on bad terms."

"And this morning, Yer Lordship, begging yer pardon," the butler put in, looking intently at the scarred snowstone table, "Siphuncle mentioned as Miss Svarabakti was interested in all kinds of fellows. He reminded her about that poet type, Fettle, and . . ."

Lord Roderick raised himself from his cushions on one elbow, frowning furiously.

"And Yer Lordship," Borcubast added innocently, "which goes to show he was so angry, he didn't care what he said at all." The old man, possibly taking refuge in the fact that butlers were hard to obtain and harder to keep, added, "Not that there mayn't have been truth in it." He dodged back into verbal safety by elaborating, "That Fettle being what he is, and that lady friend of his, Dheloris, being what she is, and Miss Svarabakti being what she was, I'm not surprised that someone left a knife in someone else. Though how I'm to serve pickled bristlefish without a proper set of knives, is more than I can say."

Lord Roderick lay back wearily and closed his eyes. Gwen and Garamond rose to take their leave. Perhaps hearing them, Usher added feebly, "Forgive me, my friends. This had been a greater shock than I would wish to admit. I must rest. Borcubast will tell you when I can speak with you again. Perhaps after dinner. Perhaps in the morning."

Roderick sighed deeply, as if even breathing cost him an effort. "And Borcubast, a drop or two of laudanum in that cordial, if you will, and ask Maudelaine to come and attend to my bandages. And, in the names of all the stars that shine upon humankind, be somewhat less forward in your speech."

21

"I never saw a house less suited for the discussion of secrets," Gwen complained. "I can't help but imagine a spy in each suit of armour or behind each arras, or at least someone around each corner, someone who shouldn't overhear whatever I'm about to say."

"Well, it's worked to my benefit already," Garamond reminded, "and it may again."

"True, but if we talk and someone else listens, it's another thing altogether." Gwen, looking carefully about, concluded that no spies lurked near the octagonal room where she and her cousin had taken refuge. Roderick Usher's door across the hall was locked, and no footfalls sounded on the nearby stairs. She sat down on a bench that had been placed so that those in the room could best admire a full-length painting of a feverish-eyed Lord Roderick leaning on a pallid bust of Pallas which he shared with a large black bird.

Garamond sat down beside her and endeavored to hold her hand. She allowed him this comfort, but counteracted it by adding, "You really didn't have to tell Lord R. quite so much about what we knew and you knew and you guessed."

"Why not?" Garamond asked simply.

"Because he could have done it."

"He couldn't do in anyone with a broken arm and a broken head and a fever."

"If," Gwen said significantly, "he has them. He could be exaggerating. If he were in serious pain, he'd surely want a more effective—if less poetic—analgesic than laudanum. But he also ought not to be told overmuch because he might be an awfully good friend of Maudelaine or Siphuncle or—what were those other things?—Fettle and Dheloris? He could tell them that people are wondering about them, and give them time to think up terribly clever stories about not being anywhere near the chapel.

And if he got the idea that we were investigating, he would throw us out. Or off the battlements."

"And," sighed Garamond, insinuating his arm around his cousin—his second cousin—"tomorrow is Threesday, and the day after that is Foursday. If we don't show up on Foursday morning with that impossible parchment before the Inspector General arrives, the governor will send us back here with a Gothic parchment of his own."

Gwen couldn't imagine the governor with a Gothic parchment, and said so.

Garamond amplified, "A letter with a medieval message such as, 'Give the bearer of this letter a firm kick off the battlements.'"

Gwen nodded resignedly, then steeled herself and rose. "In that case, we'd better get busy."

"Doing?"

"Asking. Listening. Opening things that shouldn't be opened." She turned around and gave a closer look to the bench upon which she had sat. "Get up," she ordered more firmly than was at all necessary.

Garamond looked sulky, but up he got.

Gwen put her hand to the bench seat, a seat of black and scarlet tapestry. It formed a lid and, with Gwen's expert encouragement, it opened.

As it did so, fungoid webs showed in the gap. The sight of the undulating filaments nearly caused Gwen to drop the lid. Ivory white cockades of pleated fungus encrusted the corners, exhaling a musky leaf mould odor and spreading pale tangled threads of webwork over the inner surface. At the bottom of the chest, enwrapped in arabesques of clinging tendrils, lay a skeleton. A rather fresh skeleton, but not human at all. It was the bones of a bristlefish.

22

Garamond paused on the stairway, perusing the list of persons who had been inside the manor when Borcubast had inquired shortly after the discovery of Svarabakti's body. Most of those listed were members of the household staff. The invitation list had shown thirty guests. Garamond knew of—was one of—three uninvited others. The staff consisted of fifty-three persons, most of them Kulmar.

He looked down the curve of the stairs that spiraled within the wall of a round tower. He could start at the bottom or at the top. At the top stood sentries, difficult people to question. They considered questioning to be their prerogative. Garamond didn't fancy "Who goes there?" and "What's the password?" would lead to productive casual chat.

At the bottom lay the kitchens. Homey, comfortable places to do investigation, kitchens. One gathers the staff around the jaffa pot and urges everyone to eat sweet rolls to repletion. Garamond had had opportunity to experiment with a number of truth serums and reticence relaxers. He had found nothing more effective than jaffa and pastries in a warm kitchen—though some of the more sophisticated formulas worked faster.

A footman bustled down the stairway past him. Garamond remembered that at the moment all the dining room and kitchen staff would be preparing for dinner. Hardly an atmosphere for relaxation. He sighed regretfully and began to climb the stairs.

Garamond discovered the sentry post at the top of a high central tower. Two chambers, one above the other, formed the headquarters, built when the manor was a Vonyushar fortress. From the airy upper room, unglazed window arches gazed from beneath a wickedly sharp conical roof. Here guards could see to the horizon in a circle broken only by towers of the manor itself. The only light here, a sorcerous blue glow, rose from the readout screen of the security terminal.

The stiflingly overheated living quarters directly below had walls lined with tiers of black-canvas-clad bunks and well-stocked pantry shelves. Flames darting in a deep-hooded fireplace glanced on bronze-scaled armour, polished spears, halberds, and bone-handled electrocharge blasters.

Without their armour, the Kulmar guards wore simple black waist-cloths and sleeveless black, bronze-studded undertunics. Most were pairs of identical twins, disconcerting to see with their duplication of features, all deeply tanned, golden-haired men with musculature developed in Ashpit's 1.3 standard gravities and battle-loving culture. Garamond had heard that the original human settlers on Ashpit had had a high tendency toward twinning that had increased over time to become the norm.

Identical pairs of faces watched Garamond incuriously.

"Oh, I do say." Garamond pretended the surprise of an over-curious guest, who, upon discovering a place he doesn't belong, remains to make an innocent nuisance of himself. "I say, what a jolly cubbyhole, all milit'ry shipshape and speckless. You must be the sentries, ever-vigilant staunch defenders, eh what?"

The Kulmar sentries, just off watch and divested of their half armour, still looked remarkably fierce and powerful. They sat silent on their bunks, watching Garamond incuriously as if he were an overlarge musk beetle that might cause an unpleasantness.

"You chaps must . . . I say, my apologies. In I come without introducing myself. I have to realize not everyone has an opportunity to watch the vid regularly, so I can't expect to be universally recognized."

One of the sentries groaned softly. Another whispered "actor" in Kulmar. The captain, notable by the red and gold yarn braided into his moustache and into the roll of uncut hair at the back of his neck, made a minute signal to a man sitting at the dining table. That fellow shifted his leg slightly, concealing—too late—a demijohn of Captain Kettle rum. Sentries mustn't indulge on duty days, and if their uninvited visitor was discourteous enough to stick around and tell the story of his life, he might notice this particular departure from discipline and mention it where he shouldn't.

"Yes, I'm Garamond Gray." He paused, as if for applause or at least sighs of awe. "It has been my privilege to perform the most demanding of tragic roles, and before that most demanding of audiences, Her Puissant Majesty, our Empress."

The sentries nodded loyally.

"I have been Claudius in *Claudius and Philomela*, the king in *King Henry's Folly*"—the folly had been in trying to take on the Vonyushar Empire before the support of the Glorious, Supreme, and Orgulous Oriel-Mossmarching Empire had been assured— "the Emperor in *The Dastardly Murder of Emperor Joe*, and . . . But humility bids me cease. The actor-genius must learn from all those around him. He must learn the turns of phrase of a Coromandel diving boy, the gestures of an upland brandyboar herder, in short, he must be all humanity in one. Now, I would learn from you."

The sentries hardly looked encouraging.

"Yes indeed," Garamond continued unabashed. "You chaps must be able to see nearly everything from all these turrets and towers and all. Frightfully unlucky you couldn't have seen that unfortunate murder. I saw four of your chaps nipping along to watch over the deceased. Rather a bodyguard, what?"

A few of the sentries yawned ostentatiously.

"I mean, it would have been a jolly spot of luck if you'd seen someone fleeing over the moors with gore-stained hands. I fancy all of you were on duty then. Between breakfast and luncheon as far as anyone can make out. And you didn't see anything?" He asked so wistfully, with such innocent, boyish interest in that most fascinating of subjects, the murder of someone neither near nor dear, that the sentries began to compare notes.

"I were on the south wall, lookin' over the tarn, I was," began one. "Saw nothin' better nor worse than the geese a-gawpin' an' garglin' among the sedge stalks."

" 'N' I were up above the great door, I were . . ."

Garamond, looking only mildly interested in anything but himself, took careful mental notes. The result was a confirmation of the list, as far as could be matched by numbers and general descriptions, of those revelers who had remained outside. Nothing new to be learned.

"If anyone saw anybody a-runnin' off," the captain said fairly, "it would 'a been us, 'less they ran hunkerin' through the gorse. The door wards might a-seen too. Fact is," he added with growing enthusiasm, seeing a way to rid himself of this interrupter of rest, relaxation, and rum, "if anyone left, would a' been through the door, and the door wards know all the comin' and goin'. If they be of a mind to tell."

Garamond rose to leave, negligently depositing a treasury note on the table as he passed.

Well, even negative evidence was evidence, as he had heard Gwen say all too often. He wondered vaguely if she was progressing any better.

23

Gwen, descending the stairs one flight below Lord Roderick's bedroom, and saw a familiar silvery olive tail flip secretively back from a doorway. She hurried after it to discover Hyota-ya, Kelesophos, and Patrice huddled conspiratorially in a niche incompletely covered by a silken arras.

"Hyota-ya, what have you been doing? What have all of you been doing?" Gwen had no patience for sneaking, spying, or tiptoeing by anyone but herself and her cousin.

"We've been watching for you."

"For your own safety."

"After we heard about the murder—"

"Just in case it was a Fausta feud—"

"So they sent me to listen, because I'm the lightestmost on my feet."

Gwen sorted the confused burst of information and set about attacking the vital spot. "I told you, I am not now, never have been, and never will be a member of the Fausta! I'm in no danger of a Fausta feud. Svarabakti's death probably had more to do with her love life than politics, from what I've heard. Now, is it absolutely clear? I'm not a Fausta agent. All right?"

"I . . . guess. But then why were you sneaking and whispering and all with that fellow?" Kelesophos looked puzzled in the big-eyed manner of a young snout hound that had lost a scent.

"The fellow's my cousin. We're . . . tragic actors. A team. And we've been sneaking and whispering for the same reason you have—to keep from being overheard. A lot of good it's done us."

"We didn't *really* hear anything," Hyota-ya admitted ruefully. "But we couldn't help being curious about everything." He licked the tip of his nose with an unlikely air of innocence.

Patrice, standing behind Kelesophos, hooked her hands and chin over one of his shoulders. "After all, if there's a murder in a manor house," she pointed out reasonably, "it shouldn't be any less exciting than it is on vid just because it's real and we're here.

I mean to say, it's not as if she were a friend or relation or a nice person at all."

"Besides," Kelesophos added, "she said some things the other night that might have been taken badly by any Fausta agent that might have overheard. About how the Fausta couldn't agree well enough to govern themselves."

"Lady Maudelaine said the same," Hyota-ya countered, "and no one put a knife in her."

Patrice smiled at one corner of her mouth. She added simply, "Yet."

Gwen looked at the three seriously. "How did you hear of the murder?"

"How?"

"I guess we just overheard—"

"Well, I fancy that I heard from you, Patrice, darling."

Patrice, still leaning on Kelesophos' shoulder, nibbled the side of her forefinger thoughtfully. She brightened. "I know. It was my maid. After we left you, we sort of stood around watching the revelers practice. We were supposed to practice too, but we just watched. Sort of."

"Because," Hyota-ya volunteered brightly, "a lot of people don't like Kel's dudelsack. They say it sounds like—"

"Never mind," Kelesophos interrupted.

"*So*"—Patrice regained the floor—"so when the practice was over, we came in before the others, and I went up to my room to change. I was all over damp gorse from Kel's expedition. And my maid said straightaway, 'Miss Patrice, ye wouldn't believe, we're all in a worrit and a confusification. That Svarabakti that sings with the vudu guitar fellow, she's been knifed dead, and they found her without a stitch on her but a precious necklace worth a king's ransom.'

"And she'd heard part from a footman and part from the parlour maid who was asking for something for the kitchen maid who was 'all overcome with the faints and high-steria.' So that's how we know."

Gwen sighed. "If the three of you were together . . ." The three nodded. "And were outside until the practice ended . . ." They nodded again, solemn and wide-eyed. "Then you can't have been inside when Svarabakti was killed. My cousin found the body, so we have a fair idea of the time. And it makes us even more curious than you.

"I could use your help, and I think I can trust you. Mostly

because there are three of you, so you can talk things over comfortably between yourselves without being tempted to gossip, even when everyone else is talking and conjecturing." She glanced at them questioningly.

"We'll do our best," Kelesophos said, "but I fancy there'll be any amount of talk, no matter what."

"True, but if the three of you don't tell anything new, but just repeat what you hear from everyone else, it will keep any new discoveries safe. Would you like to make some new discoveries?"

The three looked awed and eager.

"If it wasn't for finding the body like that, my cousin and I would be happy to simply sit back and conjecture with everyone else. But this makes it personal. We're involved. The way we are about the Fausta plot to capture a navy ship, because I found a bit of webwire and you explained what it meant. So we've got to do something, and we can begin by searching Svarabakti's room. Do any of you know where it is?"

They did. Back up the stairs and not too far from Lord Roderick's and Siphuncle's and Lady Maudelaine's. The very best rooms, with the largest dressing rooms and balconies and very fine paintings and tapestries. Patrice's maid had told her about them. Patrice didn't mind having one of the rooms with no dressing room because, "After all, I'm just a dancing girl. Not anyone famous, and not really expecting to be."

"But a nice dancing girl. Anyone can see that," Kelesophos consoled her, and kissed her forehead.

They climbed the stairs, Hyota-ya in the lead, walking cautiously and edging around the curve of the stairway, until Gwen had to tell him to stop. "You'd think we were spies, not houseguests. We have every right to mind Svarabakti's business for her. I never heard that she left other people's business to itself."

They reached Svarabakti's room, and Hyota-ya touched the lock plate, turning back crestfallen. "It's locked. We can't just go to the butler and ask to have it opened. Not when there has been an unusual and unexplained decease. It's simply not done."

"I'm glad someone has proper respect for official formalities," Gwen observed, coming up and testing the lock, allowing her cloak to mask her actions from her companions. "Still, we could tell old Borcubast that . . . um, that Patrice let Svarabakti borrow her new silk camisole or something, and she needs it to wear with a backless dress tomorrow night. Would that . . . ? Mercy me, but it isn't locked at all. Just stuck, I fancy. I simply jiggled the whatchamacallit, and here," she said, entering a room dark and eloquent with rich perfumes, "we are."

Svarabakti had inhabited the rooms called the Lenore Suite. Artistically draped black satin hangings covered the walls, here and there accented by a scarlet tassel, a wine red porphyry pilaster, or a gold-framed ornament. The furniture, a matching set of bed, wardrobes, chaise-longues, chairs, and writing table, all in highly polished black onyxwood, added to the funereal atmosphere. Black, too, the watered-silk hangings of the bed, fold upon fold of rustling sable draperies. Gwen flung them open. The bed lay unmade.

"What a mercy," Gwen exclaimed as her companions watched, not a little paled and subdued by their surroundings. "The maid hasn't been at the room yet. We may find any number of things we wouldn't have found otherwise."

They did. They found clothes, cosmetic stencils, vid discs of theatrical performances of types not available to minors—in several of which Svarabakti had a role—handbags, long-pile velvets (furs were not worn that season), and love letters. Well, not precisely letters, because only officialdom really wrote, and then if it couldn't help it, but decorative keepsake cards with almost illegible flourishes. Most of these seemed to read, "Darling, darling Svari—I'll never forget last night—yours forever—" at which point reason would assert itself, and the writer would only sign his initial.

As Gwen knew from previous investigations, an experienced gentleman could make his initial look like any one of a dozen letters. This calligraphic talent seemed universal among Svarabakti's correspondents.

A number of the keepsake cards enclosed rapturous offers of marriage, their blameless message bearing the writer's signature in full. Unfortunately for the investigation under way, none of these gentlemen were present at Usher's house party. Two, however, were members of Imperial Parliament whose names Gwen mentally filed for future reference.

Svarabakti's identification showed her to be a native of Khaarn-world, a politically blameless planet. It reported her profession: singer; age: twenty-six (she usually claimed to be twenty-three); and name at birth: Sally-Lu Marsh. Her wardrobe contained no flight overall emblazoned with the Fausta triple serpent, but Gwen couldn't imagine Svarabakti wearing a flight overall under any circumstances.

In the end, Patrice made the one essential discovery in Svarabakti's room. She had been searching through drawersful of, to be frank, drawers—knickers, step-ins, teddies, cami-knickers, camisoles, and Graffien Zweihoffer's Patented Uplift Antigrav Brusthalters. The wealth of lace, silk, satin, and chiffon, with and without ribbons and the odd pearl, held Patrice speechless for some time.

Once in a while when she made a particularly enthusiastic exclamation about cut, line, style, fabric, or sheer, impractical, luxurious flimsiness, Kelesophos had to remind her that she should be looking for something more significant than new fashions in knickerwear.

Under the full-length evening slips (cut down to here, and slit up to there) Patrice found a postal packet. Once a postal packet had been sealed and franked, she knew, it is a Felonious Act against Her Imperial Majesty's Mails to open it. The packet had been franked but not sealed. Not exactly. So she opened it.

It contained a thumbprint-sized disc for voice recording, and even if it recorded Svarabakti's latest effort at "Vudu Jungle Lullabye," "Three Moon Midnight," or even "The Bell Song" from *Lakmé*, why had she hidden it under her backless black satin evening petticoat?

Patrice showed her find to the other searchers.

"Good-oh!" Gwen beamed with more enthusiasm than she usually summoned for the mindless mannequin Patrice appeared to be. Nip it into Kelesophos' vambrace and we'll give it a listen."

They nipped and listened, and what transpired, though ostensibly a masterwork of the unaccompanied contralto, turned out to have a weightier message.

"Bay-ay-ay-ay-bee," sang Svarabakti's voice compellingly, "you gotta listen to me. You gotta know what I know an' see what I see."

At this point the listeners began to lose interest.

"Because I know who wrote a letter," the song continued, "that ever'body wants to read."

Gwen, riveted, tried to say, "I think that's enough of that," and eject the disc from Kelesophos' vambrace before the message went any farther.

Unfortunately, Kelesophos took that moment to raise his vambrace closer to his ear. He sat with Patrice on the foot of an onyxwood chaise longue, and Gwen sat across from him in an overstuffed chair. Thus her grasp, instead of connecting with his wrist, brought her up affectionately hugging his knee. Both he and Patrice thought it odd that so self-possessed a young woman should be sentimentally moved by such bland lyrics, no matter how expertly rendered. Patrice, in fact, considered giving Gwen a biff over the ear.

Gwen, shaken, returned to her chair in time to hear the recorded voice warble, "It means the Separatists'll have it like they want it to be."

The recording ended abruptly, leaving the four investigators looking at one another questioningly.

Gwen held out her hand. Kelesophos numbly deposited the disc in it.

"Does this mean . . . ?" Hyota-ya finally got the breath to ask.

"You're jolly well right this jolly well means what it jolly well sounds like. You three just go on as you are, hanging around and listening and nodding sapiently—I mean, as if you understand everything—while I go confer with the Venga Avest of Corbo."

24

Garamond contemplated the door wards and shook his head. He interviewed them at length, but to little avail. It appeared that they kept a close eye on everyone, but that their methods had an unconventional logic.

The twin Kulmar sentries, even taller than their two-meter colleagues, nonchalantly bore three-meter halberds and intricately engraved nerve pistols. They added beaten bronze high-crested helms and hip boots with spike spurs to the usual sentry uniform, and looked imposing indeed.

"Aye, we been watchin' who goes in and who goes out, that we have, sir. And never did we see no one goin' out after that poor lady died as didn't come in again. His butlership was one, and the governor's daughter to get her little feather wrap as she left on the bench in the glade, and the guitar chappie, out to get the governor's daughter, and the whiskery fellow as makes verses.

"He made a verse about us, sir, which we was much gratified at, though it was hardly respectful, but then, po'try's only respectful of them as is dead or on a throne, and we's neither."

Thinking his companion had waxed philosophical long enough, the other door ward, his twin, interrupted. "What the whiskery fellow made up for us, sir, was the following:

'The door guards at Lord Roddy's castle
'Attempted to give me a hassle.
      'I soon set them straight
      'With a blow to the—'"

Garamond, with a fine lack of artistic appreciation, interrupted, "So you haven't any more of a guess who did the deed than any of the rest of us? What rummy luck. You would have known," he added in a pondering manner, "if anyone had come to the house uninvited or unexpected?"

"Not a doubt to it. Why, when that Avest chap—"

"His Excellency, the Venga Avest of Corbo, as came unexpectated, but an important churchman as anyone can see," the twin explained to the annoyance of his brother.

For all the aesthetics of having a matched set of door wardens, it would be nice if they could get to the point, Garamond thought, giving them a glare which he hoped held a steely and authoritative glint.

"That Avest chap," the first guard began again firmly, "came unexpectified, but he didn't sneak out afterwards. Nothing sneaky or underhand or murderous about him."

"And when I came in," Garamond hazarded, "you knew I belonged here all right."

"That we did, sir. Saw ye nip into the line out of nowhere, and m'brother says to me—"

"The gentleman needn't hear what I says then, but I wondered a bit, that's all."

"But seein' ye was in the heraldic colours of the house, bein' black and red, what the gentry calls sable and ghouls, which is right enough in a house like this, as it's always lookin' down yer back out of its own windows and chimneys, we knew ye was invited, right enough."

"Clever fellows, you two." Garamond winked, allowing two treasury notes to appear conjurer fashion in the pouches of the door keepers. "Clever fellows indeed. Well, keep an eye open each, and see if you don't catch a felon to your greater glory and the Empire's."

The guards clicked their heels together smartly at the mention of the Glorious Empire, and by the time they had disentangled their dress spurs (a sad hazard to heel clicking) Garamond had gone.

25

Garamond shook his head again over the thought of the doorkeepers. Ever vigilant, and probably quite accurate as to whether anyone had left after the murder, but not overly B-R-I-G-H-T. (At least, Garamond *thought* there was a G-H in it, but he'd worry about that later.)

The dressing bell rang for dinner and Garamond relished the thought of a hearty splash of hot and cold before a proper dinner in the old Gothic style—perhaps roast brandy boar with a lump-fruit in its mouth—and finally questioning the kitchen and dining staff. Whatever appeared on the menu, it would make good introductory conversation with the cook.

He found his room, which had been Kennes' before, atmospherically draped with tapestries illustrating the progress of the legendary Red Death, but the door to the wash place stood closed, and sounds of splashing and snatches of song came therefrom.

"Gwen, is that you?"

"Nay, 'tis the Spectre of the Red Death," returned Gwen's voice.

"Gwen, will you hurry up? The dressing bell's rung and I want my bath."

"Right-ho. I'll just be a minute."

Garamond groaned. He had never fully grasped the time—space relativity of interstellar travel, but he knew that time is measured differently by people on opposite sides of a wash place door.

"I say, Gar, what have you found out?"

Garamond, looking up from a selection of nether hose and velvet tunics laid out by a thoughtful valet, answered briefly, "The sentries didn't see anything, but they wouldn't have seen anything anyway. The doorkeepers didn't see any fleeing murderers, but there weren't any."

"What was that? I had the water running."

"Why did you ask me a question if you were about to run the water?"

"I wish you wouldn't try to talk when I have the water on. Do you know, Gar, I found out the oddest thing. Svarabakti knew about the letter—the parchment thing. She left a message saying the letter would let the Separatists have everything their way. It was addressed to a local Fausta agent. I asked Kennes, but he had no clue she was involved."

"Well, I wouldn't mind having things my way, particularly a wash and a change before we're late for the soup."

"I said I'd only be a minute."

"That was a minute ago, Gwen." Garamond selected a black broadcloth tunic with scarlet beadwork on the shoulders. His cloak, he fancied, would cover the beadwork, which he considered overly baroque.

"What was that? I wish you wouldn't talk when the water's running."

Lord Roderick had ordered the dining room arrayed with a subtle consciousness of mourning. The vast, echoing dining hall whose barrel-vaulted ceiling rose into the shadows had a solemnity and grandeur of its own. Now, with the chandeliers dimmed and raised, and the music system wafting themes from *The Tragedy of the Planet Eschaloigne*, the atmosphere was subdued indeed.

The bouquets on the long table and the sideboards showed subdued colors, grays and burgundies shading off into deep browns against sprays of blackfern. Garamond noted the black-on-black second dynasty Coromandel place settings, appreciating the combination of style and mood they evoked. A place had been set for Lord Roderick and for Svarabakti, and the eloquence of the empty seats breathed a gloom undispelled even by the fragrance of roast goose and butterberry dressing.

The guests spoke self-consciously in the low, measured tones in which one speaks of death. Most had paid final respects in the mourning room—and most wore ostentatious black.

Siphuncle, withdrawn, kept most of his attention on his plate, eating little and giving the briefest replies decency permitted to the inevitable inquiries and offers of sympathy.

Across the table Lady Maudelaine, finding Siphuncle inattentive, turned to Kennes. The Grays heard snatches of their talk: "Nothing like this ever happened to me—Your Excellency." The girl added the title with only a touch of irony. "I mean, when Georgios crashed, well, I hadn't seen him for about a year, and besides, I never had to *look* at anything."

Kennes muttered something sympathetic and Venga Avestian.

"It was so shattering," Maudelaine elaborated. "It *was* sort of thrilling, though. Like the funeral scene from *Princess Capricia*. All those Kulmar guards with their spears and things, and her face white. It was so artistic. I rather thought—in the back of my mind, I mean—that in an hour or so she'd show up from back-stage with the white washed off, and people would congratulate her on the performance.

"But when I saw she wasn't breathing . . ." Maudelaine shuddered delicately and allowed Kennes to pat her shoulder. "They always breathe in the theater. It's so disconcerting. Remember when Pantoffle tried suspended animation serum, but it didn't wear off by curtain call? Then all of a sudden it was *real*. She was so young, really. And even if she was . . . well, anyway, she *was* a marvelous singer. And now she's down there in the dark. It's the worst thing that ever *happened* to me."

Maudelaine clutched Kennes' hand, and he held hers in both of his, trying to appear as if this were a comfort a Venga Avest would bestow.

Other guests, too, discussed the frissons the death had given them.

"I am numbed, absolutely numbed. As I told Fettle when I first heard, I cannot feel anything but the shock of it."

"You're uniquely sensitive, aren't you, Dheloris?" Fettle countered. "I can hardly say I'm surprised, considering her character, or lack of it, but it's a shock all right to see her a-cold. It's put a chill on me, somehow.

> "Svarabakti, once brimming with life,
> Met her end on a bristlefish knife . . ."*

"Don't, Fettle, please. I'll never eat bristlies again. To think I used to be fond of them—to think I had a fine, well-pickled slice this morning with no more thought as to what would happen . . . It gives me exquisite anguish."

"To me, it gives—how do you say?—the creeps."

"Cold, that's how I feel. A blizzard rages through my veins, 'til I'm as cold as she. As if with her passing, I'll never know warmth of body or soul again. Here, footman, another cup of jaffa."

With the end of dinner the guests moved into the drawing room and library where fires burned high and ruddy in huge ornate fireplaces, and attentive serving men proffered hot mulled wine and cyder.

In the drawing room Gwen turned to a handsome gray-maned actor beside her and asked confidentially, "Surely you have an idea who ... who killed Svarabakti. Why isn't anything being done?"

"Oh, but it is, milady. A list has been made of everyone who was inside the house at the time of the death. Roderick is making inquiries—inviting those people who were inside up to his room and questioning them. In the most delicate and inoffensive fashion, I understand. I, fortunately, was out on the green during the crucial time."

Dheloris lounged nearby on all of a roomy couch, while Fettle sat on the floor beside her, leaning his head back onto her lap as she stroked his hair absently. Overhearing the conversation, Dheloris tightened her grip on Fettle, making him snort exasperatedly, and asked, "When was the essential time? Dear Roddy hasn't sent for me, and I really ought to know whether I ... whether I can be of any help."

"I don't know that I ought to say." The gray-maned actor put on an importantly reticent official expression. "After all ..."

"Oh, nonsense," Gwen protested lightly. Choosing those landmarks most likely to be remembered by Dheloris, she added, "I heard it was between breakfast and luncheon. Quite a while after breakfast and shortly before luncheon. Isn't that so?"

The older man nodded noncommittally.

Dheloris laughed, and her several chins quivered with the joke. She wiped a strand of pale hair out of her eye, leaned over Fettle, almost obscuring his head with vast velvet-clad breasts, and pinched his whiskered cheeks. "Well, Fetty-wettle, are you going to tell dear Roddy where we were, or shall I?"

All of those portions of Fettle still visible blushed furiously. "Dheloris," he protested, wriggling out of her grasp, "darling," he added belatedly, "I don't think we ought ..."

His face displayed a brief catalogue of conflicting emotions that made his whiskers bristle and pivot, and he bolted from the room.

Dheloris lay back on her couch, causing it to creak, and

hugged herself with evident self-congratulation. "I have him where I want him," she exulted to the room at large.

A horrible suspicion occurred to Gwen and she looked around for Garamond, but he had slipped away some moments before.

As Gwen had witnessed in the mourning room, the drawing room assumed a solemn and oppressive mood and imposed it upon its inhabitants. Gwen felt hopeless guilt, and recounted her past sins—most of which involved circumventing officialdom in the pursuit of suspects—and wondered what she had done to deserve this overwhelming and black oppression of mind.

She looked around at a drawing room filled with people in postures eloquent of dejection, melancholy, and absolute torment. Gwen had seen enough of the house to ascertain that Usher had installed no mood-modification system. Apparently one as sensitive as he desired none of the psychotrophic euphoriants fashionable in some circles. Though efficiently computerized, the house did not have a self-aware system. Evidently, Lord Roderick, having decided on the luxury of human servants, had not wanted a house system with other than merely practical electronics.

The oppressive sense of guilt and despair lifted slightly, and those who had been tearing their hair ceased and looked around them with some vestige of hope.

"Listen!" Little silver-haired Yin, curled tightly in the cubby under a writing desk, raised her head and spread her jug-handle ears to their fullest extent. "Can you hear them? Spirits, whispering and piping, small and shrill as—what is it you say?—as flittermice in a brick silo. They want something. They ask a question, but I cannot understand." Her eyes grew large and she seemed ready to weep, striving to catch the transient sounds.

Yotu looked up from a page he had been illustrating directly after dinner, and which, under the recent oppressive influence, he had been carefully tearing into neat, narrow strips. "I hear it too —no—yes. But it fades. It must be too high a pitch for human ears." He made a general bow to the unfortunate humans. "It seemed to ask urgently—some question I couldn't grasp. It's gone." Yotu sighed, wiped his nose delicately on his black lace neckerchief, and subsided back onto a cushion on the floor.

In the following moment of silence, during which the humans wondered what the two Shardé had heard, if they had heard anything at all, the door from the hall creaked open. Its hinges seemed designed to give Gothic punctuation to suspense-filled silences.

In staggered Lord Roderick, his face chalky and his eyes dilated with laudanum, fever, and fear. He clutched at the doorpost for support with skeletal fingers trembling. A matched pair of twin footmen leaped to support him. As they reached him, he fell forward into their arms, almost tearing free from their grasp in the utter collapse of an exhausted swoon.

*Fettle's limericks appear in complete form in the Appendix.

26

Garamond crept away from the discussion in the drawing room and descended wide, mirror-polished stairs to the dining
room. From there, following his nose through passages narrow,
rough-hewn, and unornamented, he arrived at the kitchen.

Steamy, savoury smelling, brightly lit, the kitchen combined
stone floors and vaulted ceilings with computer linked micro-
waves, culinary preprocessors, freezing and controlled environ-
ment pantries, waste vaporization units, and the house's fusion
generator (tucked under a Frankenhauser butcher table). Two
fireplaces blazed merrily, their radiance reflecting on an array
of kitchen implements as bright and fine-honed as the swords in
the sentry hall.

Kitchen staff, footmen, and servitors sat around a long table,
at the head of which sat the cook, as dignified as a duchess. All
but the lingering fragrance of gorse goose and butterberry dressing had vanished, but the group remained dawdling over jaffa,
cream cake, and the remains of mulled cyder.

"Well, then." The cook used a soupspoon as a gavel to call her
people to order.

Garamond drew back from the archway to listen invisibly.

"Now then, that was done proper, and my thanks and his lordship's for the doing of it. A substantial dinner with no frills or
flambustiousness, but not so downright solemn as to keep folk
from eatin' of it. That's that his lordship asked for, and I daresay
it's what we projuiced. Goes to show ye can pay as fitting respect
for them as passed over with proper food, service, and tableware
as with bellowin' and knee-callusing in the chapel. Not to speak
poorly of priests and saints, though thin and feeble eaters they
seem to be."

"Not that Bendy Abest, though," asserted a maid lately put in
charge of the jaffa making on the sideboard and feeling rather
superior in consequence.

"The Venga Avest of Corbo?" the cook corrected delicately.

"Yes, he seems to have more than a holy man's appreciation of what goes on a plate."

"My eggs... the cormorant eggs..." A fledgling kitchen maid spoke up with worshipful gratitude that the Venga Avest had chosen those eggs she had providentially discovered—and relapsed into abashed silence.

The cook smiled on her with concerned affection. "That's a good girl. You'll check that nest in the morning, belike? But run along to bed early. You don't look well. Is it one of your headaches a-comin' on?"

The girl shook her head and covered her face with trembling fingers, trying to stifle a sob.

The inquisitive footman Brennu stood to clear his place, shook his head sympathetically, and said under his breath, "You never know where you are with a tripling like that." The serving maids within hearing nodded and sighed their agreement. At that point Garamond slipped in.

"I'm so glad, so deuced jolly glad, that I got here before you people were all in a bustle, steaming the naperies and vaporizing the goose bones, or whatever goes on after you've had your morsel of goose." He brought a chair up to the table, the footman sat down again, and an expectant silence reigned. The appearance of Lord Roderick's guests in the kitchen often caused a delay and a nuisance, but seldom failed to be entertaining.

"And a very fine flock of geese they were," Garamond continued, as if he had nothing more on his mind than hearing himself speak, and as if his audience could have no objection as long as he continued to compliment them. "Geese are fat creatures, which makes them so cunning to watch, but the fat must be broiled out of them, and they must come to the table sizzling, as there's hardly a more depressing taste than cold fat in poultry. There was surely none of it tonight."

"Why thank you." The cook inclined her head slightly. "I'm glad you found things to your taste."

"Oh, I did, I did. Don't you fancy that the gorse these birds eat adds a honey-bright touch to their flavor? My grandfather used to fancy them especially, not only for the taste, but because the geese and gorse, like himself, had a Terran ancestry, although they were developed to their present excellence in Coromandel's temperate zone."

Again the cook inclined her head graciously. She motioned for a footman to pass a tankard of mulled cyder and glanced aside to see the kitchen maid still all atremble. In an attempt to prevent the gentleman seeing the little lass in one of her moody fits, the cook looked Garamond firmly in the eye and explained that they raised their own geese. "Free range, with no fencing or clipping, and his lordship has parties to hunt the ground wolves and cattylions that prey on geese and snouters."

Garamond understood the cook's fixed expression, glanced around to see what she didn't want him to notice, and observed only a kitchen maid on the verge of tears, not a bloodied fish knife or a vial of poison.

"And you use your own cormorants too, I understand," Garamond added, "freshwater cormorants in the tarn? And fish no doubt. Let me guess: whiskerlings, tail-floats, and rosy-nosers? But bristlefish, needing seawater or brackish inlets at the least, you import pickled?"

The kitchen maid's eyes grew bulgingly round, and she interlaced her fingers over her mouth to keep herself quiet. The cook looked hardly less shocked and drew herself up. "We have bristlies portaged in—in the early morning so his lordship doesn't hear the aircar flying to and from the portage hatch—but for anyone to suggest that we fly them in pickled! Why, *we* do that ourselves"—she might have been using the royal *we*—"with our own cyder vinegar, fennel, bitterberry, and sedge seed."

"No, really?" Garamond feigned amazement. "I wouldn't have offended his lordship's kitchens for the world, but what trouble you must be put to, to pickle enough bristlies for this many guests at every breakfast."

"Oh, we have no slackers in my kitchen—his lordship's, I should say. But his lordship often has fifty guests for the High Days, the hunting, or if he's doing amateur dramatics. And we don't just feed the sentries and staff on mealie grub and water. Not that we'll have bristlies again this visit, after—Poika be merciful—what's happened this day."

Garamond drained his tankard with finality. "I say, was that knife that killed the lady the same that the Lady Maudelaine, um, had at breakfast? She must be quite shaken at the coincidence."

"Now, was it?" The cook looked around the table, and her staff looked back at her, earnestly awaiting a signal as to what to say. "Now, I saw it in her ladyship's hand, but did I see her put it down at all? Did any of you see anything? We may as well say what we know. *We're* all innocent, thank the saints."

The kitchen maid drew in a breath like a sob, covered her face, and sniffed hopelessly as tears seeped between her fingers.

"You never know," the footman repeated confidentially to Garamond. "You never know where you are with a tripling. Moodly and ailsome and terrible nervous, but they're good luck, as you may have heard, and three live as cheap as twinlings." The truisms drew nods all round the table.

"Ah." Garamond sighed understanding. Not that it explained the young maid's fears and tears tonight. He recalled that though the Kulmar often have twin children, from time to time they have triplets, and place superstitious significance on such a birth. One of the three is usually a weak, unthriving creature, seemingly a biological afterthought to the other two hearty, identical children. In the old days, Garamond understood, these triplings had been seen only as a burden, and likely as not were dropped off the rocks for the storm birds.

In the better economy of the Imperial times, when the market for twin guards and servitors reached as far as the stars, triplings took on a new significance. They hired out with their stronger siblings as a part-price bonus, and as compensation for low pay and small quarters, were made much of in the servants' wing, cosseted and spoiled and fed dainties. As a result, they tended to live longer in offworld service than they would on the harsh steppes of Ashpit, but their ways and weaknesses had become a matter of proverb.

But what, Garamond wondered, *could a red-eyed, shivering, pale little mite like that know about a fatal fish knife?*

The weaknesses of triplings tended more toward dropping crystal when startled, taking the wrong clothes to the wrong room (Garamond had once been supplied with the complete regalia of a Nilga-Harzha archbishop by a tripling valet), and weeping at any harsh word. "I say," Garamond began, trying to avoid alarming the overwrought girl, "surely someone knows something of the knife—or knives."

Faced with two rows of shrugged shoulders and puzzled rubbings of noses and clearing of throats, Garamond took another angle. "Now, after Lady Maudelaine left the breakfast room, did anyone take breakfast up to her?"

"Ah, that I did surely." The young woman who spoke, creamy haired, dark eyed, sturdy, large of nose but not uncomely, looked slightly familiar. On second glance, Garamond recognized her as one of the twin maids in charge of the jaffa pot at breakfast. On third sight, she was also sister to the tripling.

"That I did. She rang for tea, just sweetstraw tea with no cream to it. But I'd heard in the kitchen what had happened between those ladies, and I didn't like the thought of a young lady all shaken and angry-like, going through the morning with no more ballast for her belly bone than straw tea. So up I took her a millet loaf, sausage, and a roast apple, with a pot of cream on her tea tray."

"That was very thoughtful of you," Garamond complimented, reminded once again that Kulmar servants tend to go beyond mindless obedience.

"Oh, Marli's a good girl, she is," the footman Brennu commented indulgently.

"And when you got to her room," Garamond asked, "did you see that knife anywhere about?"

The maid thought for a while, and Garamond didn't coax or coach her. "Not a bit of it. If I'd seen it, I'd have brought it away, surely. The only knife I left her was a conserve knife for citron marmalade. As blunt as a bheer barrel, I assure you."

"Of course," the footman Brennu pointed out, "if, and I only mean *if*, Lady Maudelaine had meant to do ill with that knife, she'd have tucked it away with her stockings." Nods and murmurs of agreement followed his statement.

"Then," Garamond proposed, "what about Svarabakti? Who took her breakfast to her? Did she have a knife?"

In the following silence, the servants furrowed their brows and looked questioningly at one another.

"Why, I don't think she had breakfast at all," exclaimed the maid who had served Lady Maudelaine. "She wasn't in her room when I took breakfast to the uncle." She saw Garamond's puzzlement. "You must know who I mean. He's ever so famous, but he has such a queer name. The neoclassical guitarist from Shamal."

"Siphuncle!" half the table chorused.

"Of course. He'd asked for quite a lot of fresh fruit and sweet muffins—offworld fruit he wanted, from the tropics with those odd names, though he said . . . But yer wanting to know about the knife and the lady. Well, when I got to his door, I heard a rousting and a raucousing, and I didn't know whether to go in or put the tray on the table outside. But knowing what I do of human nature, when ye interrupt a pair of quarrelers, they'll stop and make like all is well till ye leave, and I thought if they stopped and got their breath, perhaps they'd leave off their foolishments."

The maid glanced around the table to see how much more narrative her audience could encompass, and wisely came to her point. "In I went, trying to be as inconspectacle and innocent as you please, and who was promisin' him a knife in the mornin' and the underpits after but Svarabakti who might, Poika forbid, be fricasseein' in those pits herself? And who was tellin' her that he'd throttle the breath from her and hang her up for the roaks to peck at if she laid ill hand or ill word on him or the governor's daughter but that Siphuncle?"

"Did they see you?" Garamond asked.

"Maybe so and maybe no, but it didn't matter to them, so hot in their words not to stop for mere maids or fresh lumpfruit. I heard all that in the time that I neared the door, made up my mind, put the tray in the room, and got beyond hearing. I'm not one to hasten by when there's such hearty listenin', but I had a busy morning ahead and daredn't loiter."

"Well," said Garamond, running both hands back through his rich fluff of pale hair, hardly disarranging it. "Well, that is interesting. Now, as for his lordship . . ."

As if long primed for this question, the talkative footman and the informative maid began at once, "There's no way he—" "I was there all the time—" They stopped, glanced at one another, blushed, glanced back at the tabletop, looked up again, and shrugged. The footman made way for the maid with a gesture.

"That's why I had such a busy morning. Borcubast—that's the butler—told me that someone had broken a pitcher in the hall outside his lordship's room. It had left a lot of damage, and I was to tend to it."

"Near the octagonal room?" Garamond asked.

"The room with eight sides and a painting of the master?" The maid blushed again. "No, on the other side of the stairs from that. It was clear in a minute that someone had thrown the pitcher, thrown it right hard, and it wasn't full of water, but lumpfruit nectar, which stains ever so bad. No one was free to clear it away until the breakfasts had been taken up, so as soon as I'd left the last one, I started in. Brennu was kind enough to lend a hand"— she glanced up shyly at the footman—"and we bleached and polished for ever so long, right outside Lord Roderick's room, and never he came out, nor never we went in."

"There he stayed all the mornin'," the footman amplified.

"Though it's near treason that we should even think he needed clearing of murder, cold or hot. I had just seen Marli there, when out comes Borcubast and says his lordship's fevered and groanful, and not to be nursed or waited on or tiptoed around unless he rang for it. That's the way it is with his lordship—can't abide fuss when his nerves are feeble."

"And clean and clear we did all mornin'," the maid put in, "until Borcubast came back with the tragical report, and every so often we'd hear his lordship groan or pace about the floor or shuffle with the things in his desk, and whenever he'd groan, we'd look at each other and wonder should we go in, but we knew he had his bells by his bed and by his couch, and we hardly cared to have him all in a fever shouting us out from where we weren't wanted."

"That sounds clear enough," Garamond said, still pondering this report. "But about that knife . . .?"

Borcubast entered the kitchen archway, looked around him, and reached as if to take a seat. He might not have been the butler, but Saint Richard and Saint Charles in one, to see the little kitchen maid, the tripling.

She rocketed from her seat with a wail, threw herself upon Borcubast like a ground wolf on a woolly snouter, and sobbed in utter hopelessness, "Save me! Save me! I didn't mean to do it. I'm only a poor tripling, and I get mixy in the memory, but I never meant to do such a thing till I saw it was done and the knife in my hand. By Saint Richard's thumb, I never meant it, and I'll never eat a bristlie again if I'm saved from the punishment I deserve."

"What in the world?" Garamond asked the kitchen staff at large, but received no answer. The servants crowded around the hysterical tripling, and the last Garamond saw of her, she rolled up her eyes to a frightening extent, emitted a long wail that fell into silence, and clung passionately to Borcubast as he carried her away.

Looking after the elderly butler trembling even under the slight weight of the girl—and looking proud of the burden—the footman sighed philosophically, glanced back at Garamond, and pronounced, "You *never* know where you are with a tripling."

27

Once certain that he wouldn't learn anything from the little kitchen maid until she had slept off her hysteria—or even then, as Borcubast seemed ready to protect her against all comers —Garamond whistled his way upstairs to the drawing room. It stood empty, with the fire burned down to jewellike coals on the hearth.

Almost empty. Garamond heard soft whisperings in the Shardé tongue and would have passed by except for the phrase, "Drive out those unfashionable oppressors."

Garamond edged around the door and stepped, light-footed, where he could see. The glow from the fireplace gave enough light—enough that Garamond sidestepped along the wall, not to be silhouetted in the doorway.

Quite near the fire, on a fine Ghorreck carpet woven in the old-style cloud-serpent pattern, lay Yotu and Yin, side by side on their backs, their arms cushioning their heads, and the flexy tips of their tails clasped lovingly.

"... for our chief to write *such* a letter," Yotu whispered, "much less leave it where I could find it. *Surely* only duty prompted that I take it to the governor—before our chief could sober himself and burn it."

"And have you found it here?" Eyes dancing with mischief, Yin whispered excitedly. "Have you found it? Will it *truly* bring the navy?"

"Only blood can wash out such an affront to the Empress as is in his letter, marked with his name, his sign, and his nose-print. Or so the parliament and the navy will say to gain merit with the silly sow who sits the throne. But when the navy comes into Shardé skies ..."

"*Only* a light cruiser or two to frighten us into obedience," Yin continued, like a child reciting a well-loved bedtime story.

"And the cruisers are taken by the so-aesthetic Fausta ..." Yotu chuckled in his red side-whiskers. "We will have Imperials to ransom to the Empire for the price of our independence, and the Fausta will have a cruiser for their enrichment and ours. And all through the cleverness of one who gifted our chief with plum brandy and waited to see what would come forth." Yotu thumped his chest, punctuating the proud purr echoing therein.

"But by whose work," Yin's whisper quavered a little, "did a Fausta agent die this day, when none but we should have known what she was?"

Yotu cradled Yin's head on his breast, tenderly stroking her silver cheek tufts. "Is that what worries my silver jewel, my most precious revolutionary? Did you think I had done such a thing, even had a Fausta turned traitor? But she stayed faithful—to the cause. No traitor she—-but to men. She died for that unfashionable passion-jealousy of humankind, surely, and our plot and plan is known to none. In the morning I will take the letter from its too-amusing hiding place, and you and I shall return to the City of Fountains and meet with that Fausta agent who will make the best use. But for now, show me that new game you spoke of, and we will leave the Empire be until morning."

Garamond, head whirling in hopes of making sense of all he had heard, whisked silently away. Svarabakti a Fausta agent? Too farfetched. But who better than a renowned singer of whom everyone would say, "Too farfetched," and whose bookings took her here and there throughout the Empire—and who could change destinations at the drop of a temperament. He had to think . . .

An hour later he padded into his room, that which had been Kennes' before, and eased himself silently into bed. He nudged Gwen out of the middle of the mattress, confirmed in his suspicion that the bigger the bed, the more room she took up.

She sat up, tousled but instantly alert, to say, "Just after you left the drawing room, it changed mood, like the mourning room did."

"It wasn't my fault."

"Did the rest of the house change?"

"Not the parts I was in. I can't speak for much but the kitchens."

"Yin and Yotu said they heard a high-pitched whispering— spirits, they called it—but it faded away. The next thing we knew, Lord Roderick came staggering in at the door, white as death, and collapsed before saying a word. The footmen carried him out, and Borcubast came down not long after to say that Lord

R. was all right, just feverish and exhausted, but sleeping well when he left."

"It must be Borcubast's night for dealing with the swoons." Garamond added his story, punctuated with yawns, and lay snoring discreetly before the end of it, leaving Gwen to wonder, as he had, if Svarabakti had truly been a Fausta agent, and if so, how that could have brought about her death.

III

Threesday

*Wherein those Innocent and Otherwise
Confuse Matters Personal and Imperial*

28

In the morning, most of Lord Roderick's guests rang for breakfast in their rooms, desirous of avoiding eyes that glanced from one to another and the almost audible thoughts: *I wonder if he . . . Could she have . . . ? Who has done this thing? Whom can I trust?*

In the sparsely used breakfast room, nodding to acquaintances, plying their forks with a flourish, Gwen and Garamond tucked into eggs, sausage, pastry, and spiced jaffa with a heartiness that made some of the other guests flinch and turn away. Dressed alike in tights, knee tunics, and hip cloaks all of black, in fabric that flowed dramatically to second their every gesture, instead of looking ominous or funereal or like the tragic actors they pretended to be, they looked sleek, fit, and overenergetic. If they had leapt up and called on everyone to come down to the tarn for a brisk dip or a bit of rowing, no one would have been surprised.

If anyone looked half as lively as they, it had to be Siphuncle. If anyone should have been moping in solitude, mourning or feigning to mourn, making life a burden for the servants, and casting gloom on anyone who saw him, it should have been Siphuncle. His black velvet robe, sprucely brushed; his tawny beard, combed to perfection; his affectation of a graddy skull, today worn in the middle of his forehead on a leather thong—all spoke of well-being and delight in life. His eyes twinkled, and he matched Fettle line for line in inventing a space chantey for sailors long from planetfall:

"The captain's the son of a bachelor," Siphuncle caroled lustily, beating time with a cream bun.

"And the helmsman's the son of a slug." Fettle looked to have slept badly, but seemed determined to make the most of the morning.

"And the rest of the crew, except me and you, they must ha' found under a rug."

Garamond looked away from this image of jolly camaraderie

to seek the butler. He found him adding the final flourishes to a piece of advice to a footman loading a breakfast tray, waited for the footman's departure, and asked confidentially, "I say, what about that Yotu chap?"

"He's having whitefruit and creamed barley in his room," the butler answered simply, then added under his breath, "with no sign of leaving or packing, and his face at half mast." Returning to his normal voice, he added, "The farmers to the south bring in our whitefruit by mule. Cheaper than portage, they say. Perhaps ye'll be able to see their picturesque caravans durin' yer stay."

"That would be a jolly sight, what? I hope good old Yotu doesn't miss it, fond of whitefruit as he is and all."

"I will certainly let ye know, sir, if there's anythin' of interest at the main gate." The elderly retainer bowed, allowing the suggestion of a wink to hover at the corner of one eye.

"There, now"—Garamond turned back to Gwen—"that should give us some breathing time. You can see to this and that, while I see to the other."

Gwen inclined her face close to Garamond, over a tray of jellied grass orchids. "Be careful, Gar," she warned in an undertone.

"Don't worry about me, old thing. I'll be all right."

Gwen rolled her eyes. "Not you, the investigation. If anything goes wrong now, we won't have a chance to get it back under control before Inspector General Carp has his nose in it. We've got a day left, and more ends to tie up than a Coromandel cord weaver. At least we can trust Borcubast to watch Yotu, can't we?"

"I daresay. I think he takes a fatherly interest in keeping me out of trouble. He seems to think I'm overrich and not overclever." Garamond's tone changed unexpectedly. "I'm not really stupid, am I, old dear? Not really?"

His cousin gave him a brief squeeze. "You're certainly clever enough to act daft when you need to. No vacuum dome can do that. But we'll congratulate ourselves when we have everything in order. Unless we want a jellied orchid, we'd better run along."

Garamond who had never eaten an orchid, waved Gwen away encouragingly and, once her back had turned, appropriated a flower. He had the disappointing sensation of eating perfumed tissue paper in sweet glaze, left half his orchid on his plate, and drifted over toward Siphuncle.

Fettle sang with carefree abandon, ". . . by a meteorite from the northern pole, so we drew lots to fill the hole."

"And when we landed in Joshburg-town, we turned the bawdy house upside down," Siphuncle chorused, and called Fettle's attention to the approach of Dheloris.

That lady, having breakfasted thoroughly in the quiet of her room, and having meditated on matters touching herself and one Fettle, came forth with the Olympian authority wielded only by those vast of girth and strong of will. She uttered no word, but looked, only looked, from Fettle to Siphuncle and back. The chantey died on their lips. Siphuncle might be a star in the firmament of popular music, but to Dheloris, a musician in her own right, he shrank to being one of Fettle's low companions the moment she needed Fettle.

She laid no hand upon him, but by Fettle's bearing as he departed in her wake, she might as well have dragged him by the ear. As he left, Garamond slid into his chair.

"Ah, Siphuncle, I believe? I'm Garamond Gray. You might have seen me doing *Claudius* in *C. and Philomela* on Moss-marching, Khanidar, and Baldkopf. A ripe bit of work that is—a part to tear a cat in—but why am I talking about myself? I've seen a few of your shows—not counting vid, though most do—and I fancy you jolly well put your Shamalite twelve-string through its paces."

Garamond beamed so innocently, extended his hand so winningly, that Siphuncle, who would normally have shuddered in furious silence at such a self-introduction, found himself shaking the proffered hand with bonhomous warmth.

"That large female—what is it she does? Stone drums?" Garamond continued with the semblance of naive good-fellowship, "She seems to have quite a hold over the whiskery chap. Poor fellow. I'd hate to be in her clutches. Might get lost among her chins. But I beg your pardon, they're surely friends of yours, and it's never done to make the ha-ha over someone's physiognomy. After all, no matter how often this, my native set of features, has graced the vid, tricked out in paints, horse whiskers, and all the trappings of dramatic art, few recognize me, and not all would find me handsome."

Siphuncle laughed and clapped his new companion on the back. "Come out on the battlements and have a breath of air," he said, leading the way to the stairs. "If we're going to be outspoken of our neighbors, we must rise above them—at least to the nearest tower top—and say our say out of hearing."

They emerged on the sunlit top of one of the lower towers,

which, though capped with a conical roof, had a full circle of arched, unglazed windows letting in light and air.

So disarmingly naive and good-hearted did Garamond appear that he attracted confidences. Strangers spoke to him as they would confide in a dog or graddy, which, understanding hardly a word, would still look up sympathetically and wave its tail in solemn semblance of comprehension.

"Yes, poor old Fettle seems changed for the worst," Siphuncle pondered aloud, leaning his folded arms on the stone windowsill. The Gothic setting and the graddy skull on his forehead would have made him look quite sorcerous if it weren't for the sunlight and his evident good spirits. "It's as if that hippopotamoid female had a hold over him. It came over him between morning and night yesterday. I wouldn't like to think it of them, but the word blackmail comes to mind; and if there's a reason for it—I shouldn't say it—there was a murder yesterday, after all."

"Oh, I say," Garamond protested vaguely. To Siphuncle's ears it might have been the barking of a graddy.

"Oh, I'm not saying it's likely, but if she's been chivvying and jiggoting the poor fellow for the wedding bells and the vine-covered cottage, and he's been disporting himself with dear old Svarabakti, may she rot in peace . . ." The wince of bitterness in his voice passed in a moment, and he went on, rubbing his forefinger back and forth on his moustache.

"I don't say she did more than flirt with poor Fettle—Svarabakti, I mean—but she said a few things, and he said a few things, and one thing leads to another. So if they'd had words— and I'd like to know who knew Svara without having words with her—and he did her quietus make with a bare bodkin, and Dheloris got suspicion of it . . . Or even if it didn't happen and she got the suspicion, and he couldn't clear himself, well . . . Well, there he'd be on his knees on the hearth rug, saying, 'Wilt thou be mine, and I shall cherish thee as long as thou speakest not of where I was on Twosday between the hours of bruncheon and luncheon.'"

Garamond withdrew from the next window over to look at Siphuncle with such liquid eyes in so unlined a face as might never have had a care in the world. He apparently thought nothing but good of everyone and couldn't be convinced of ill will if he stood up to his chin in it. "You don't really think that, what? I mean, you don't really think she was a bad girl, do you now?"

It seemed restful to Siphuncle to explain the iniquities of

Savarabakti to this young actor chap. He couldn't take any harm from listening—he'd simply disbelieve what he didn't want to believe. How had he ever come to act without any knowledge of human nature? That Garamond now performed his most successful role never occurred to Siphuncle.

". . . So," he summarized, "that's how she was. Took what she wanted, kissed you on the cheek, said, 'Now, please, I implore you not to be a nuisance,' and was sitting on the next fellow's lap before that last kiss dried. If anyone had done the same by her, she'd have rocked the stars on their moorings with her fury, but she wouldn't understand.

"It happened to me—I who was footloose and heart-free until I saw her—when we had half a year's engagements yet to do. I knew who she was and what she was, but we began talking marriage and similar nonsense. One night she didn't come in. Just before we went on stage the following night she simply appeared—we'd been in a frenzy looking for her. She ran up to me and gave me that final kiss. She was 'so sorry,' but there was someone else. Someone! My friend. My mentor. I'd learned in the shade of his dread-cane tree on Tabu—learned most of what I know. He came on our tour, an old, sleepy, backworld man, just for the fun. For the fun.

"Night after night, Svara and I jammed and jived and joie-de-vivred before audiences that didn't know we hardly spoke anymore offstage."

Siphuncle shook his head. He stretched, reached up to the point of the arch of the window, and playfully tapped at a web of fungus trailing across the opening. It drew hastily back, forming a nondescript clot. Tentatively, almost coyly, it reached out tendrils again, drew back from human touch, and stretched out exploratory tendrils once more.

"Odd stuff, that," Siphuncle mused, and turned back to look over the tarn and the countryside, the quarreling of pootocks over a poot hen, the grouching of geese, and his memories.

"My old mentor—it nearly killed him when she played the game on him. He went home to his dread-cane tree and his little house made of jungle stuff and cattle bones. Once in a while he rides five keem on a water cow to the trans office to call me and we talk about old times, and he never mentions her name.

"Then it was another singer, a boy with three hairs to his beard, then—then it was the manager of the Mossmarching Metropolitan Opera. For the first time, a man who could give—or withhold—more than she could. You know how much opera means these days, and for all Svara had become, if she had starred with the Mossmarching Metropolitan—ah, what she would have been then. In good conscience, love or lust aside, he couldn't give her a starring role, and no role above the chorus until next season. She raged, she wept—but she still had the few weeks of our tour to do. She swept out of the manager's office at the Metropolitan like the grande dame she nearly was—and came back to me. Until Lord Roderick. Until Fettle. Until, for all I know, she had broken the hearts of everyone from the boot boy to the sentry captain, not forgetting old Borcubast.

"When Lady Maudelaine arrived, it was refreshing to be sought after by someone so transparent and uncomplicated. A spoiled girl with the simple desire for more spoiling. We took some pleasure together, she and I, and laughed at Svara's fury. I didn't think that daddy's little Muffin had the pluck she showed, standing up to Svara at breakfast, with the blood still on her face, holding that knife and having the sense not to use it. Because of that, I know she didn't use it later on. She'd had the chance and all the reason she could have, and held back. She wouldn't have made the mistake of killing."

"But Svarabakti wasn't really bad, was she?" Garamond asked, large-eyed, as if he had hardly heard a word. "I mean, she was beastly fickle and all that, but I daresay she only thought it was a bit of fun."

For a moment Siphuncle wondered if the graceful, dark-haired woman who had breakfasted with young Garamond behaved so disgracefully to him, dismissing it as a "bit of fun."

"What I mean is, she's not the sort who would be a traitor to the Empire or something like that, what?"

Siphuncle wondered whether Garamond was even more simpleminded than he thought.

"I mean, I'm going about this the wrong way, but if someone said she was an agent for the Fausta, well . . . ?" Garamond pressed.

"Svarabakti? You must be mad!"

"Well, I was moping around, not paying any attention last night, and I overheard one of these Shardé fellows. A Separatist. He was going on about some plot—just politics." Garamond spoke with the disdain of the ignorant for mere politics. "And he said Svarabakti was a Fausta agent, but he didn't think that was why she was murdered."

"My dear chap, I think you must have misunderstood. Svarabakti had no more understanding of politics than you . . . than your average snout-herder," Siphuncle amended hastily. A cloud came under the sun, and a sensation of cold not entirely of the weather seemed to breathe from the stones into the hearts of the men. "She had nothing to do with Shard beyond a few friendships—men—including the governor of Kettlewharf. She said she'd had some fun once with that Fausta pilot, Georgios, but what had she to gain from the Separatists or the Fausta?"

Garamond sighed relief. "I didn't fancy," he said with impersonal innocence, "that you were involved in the political end of it. The Separatist, Yotu, didn't think she died for her politics. He thought she died because of human jealousy. And who would have been more jealous than—"

Siphuncle leaped at Garamond quicker even than Garamond expected. As he ducked under Siphuncle's arm, Siphuncle caught him by the collar of his cloak and threw him back against the wall.

"What do you mean? Who are you to be asking questions?"

As Garamond edged aside, Siphuncle lunged again. Garamond kicked out at him, missed, felt Siphuncle's hands on his shoulders, felt a cold rim of stone against his back. His eyes must have closed for a moment; he opened them to see gray, wind-tumbled clouds below him, and above him, cloud-shadowed moors and the dull pewter surface of the tarn.

He kicked out again, but guardedly. *Every action*, he thought, *has an equal and opposite reaction. And as long as I'm struggling half over the edge of this beastly windowsill at the top of this unlikely tower, I don't want to be the one responsible for tipping me over the edge.*

29

Gwen established herself in Lady Maudelaine's room by force of personality. Knowing that one strong-minded woman knows another—and usually loathes her—Gwen assumed a more benign guise.

"Oh, pardon me, I thought this was Garamond's room," Gwen explained, abashed, when Maudelaine opened to her insistent knocking. Hardly glancing at the girl's childish pout and lowering brows, Gwen rushed past her, exclaiming, "Oh, what is that? Where did you get it?"

Gwen grasped avidly at a toy for the fashionable child-woman of the day, a stuffed, plush pootock, scale-feathered, beaded, sequined, with rounded figure, knowing eye, and ingratiating smile on its fat beak.

Lady Maudelaine had hardly gotten her breath to protest when she found Gwen curled up on her divan, oblivious to her, rocking the pootock ecstatically in her arms. Maudelaine could be ungracious, and say, "Please begone, I wish to be alone." She could be overgracious, and say, "That's Warbert. Do take him, you love him so, but please begone, I wish to be alone." She had no intention of giving up little Warbert, and dared lose no friends by appearing ungracious. She wanted to be alone because she didn't dare talk to anyone, not even Siphuncle who seemed too heartlessly untroubled. Not even Kennes. Yet. But this stranger hardly seemed likely to understand anything more complex than pootocks, and toy ones at that.

Lady Maudelaine sat gingerly on the edge of a tawny gold stuffy chair, ready to leap to open the door if her unwelcome guest showed any signs of leaving. "Hullo," she said tentatively. "That's Warbert. Siphuncle gave him to me. He called in to Kettlewharf for someone to bring him in the morning with the f-fish." She faltered on the fatal word.

Gwen looked up with a perkily self-centered smile. "Oh, I'm *so* sorry." She looked as though she had never been sorry in her life, and in her tone and glance, Lady Maudelaine saw a chilling reflection of herself. Maudelaine determined that if she survived all this, she would drop any affectations that reminded her of this spoiled chestnut-haired creature.

"... *so* sorry. I'm Gwen Gray. You probably know my name. I'm an actress with the ... Oh, you're Lady Maudelaine, the governor's daughter, from Kettlewharf."

Lady Maudelaine, who already knew who she herself was, only nodded coldly.

Gwen crossed her legs comfortably, lovingly perched the pootock on her knee, and looked up with engagingly vacant good humour. "It's so smashing to meet someone nice," she bubbled. "Everyone here rather looks at one as if ... Well, as if one shouldn't be here unless one's ancestors came out on the first slowboat or one owns a couple of worlds or so. I mean, it's not enough to have performed before crowned heads, unless the crowned heads requested one's return for a command performance. And, well, you know, they didn't. But you're not like that. And I just adore Warbert. You said Siphuncle got him in Kettlewharf? Oh"—her face fell—"but he'd be a one of a kind."

"I could ask Siphuncle."

"Oh, would you? Could you introduce me to Siphuncle? I think he's just the absolute most, and I've been dying to tell him, but I haven't got the ... I'm too shy. Besides, Garamond would simply kill me. Garamond's my cousin. Kissing cousin, you know?"

"I know. I saw him with you last night at dinner. A tall chap with fluffy pale hair, long face, and big, brown eyes?"

Gwen nodded, all smiles.

"Certainly, I can introduce you to Siphuncle, only"—Maudelaine saw Gwen merely looking expectant, apparently oblivious to any finer shades of mood or meaning—"only he's under a bit of a strain now, you know." Gwen seemed to need reminding. "After what happened yesterday." Gwen nodded solemnly as an owl. "So he's under a bit of a strain." Maudelaine fancied Gwen must be one of the sort, like a number of her friends, to which things had to be explained twice.

Gwen returned innocently, "He looked all right at breakfast. Oh, he ate a big plateful of fruit salad and things, and ..." Her brow contracted with the effort of a quarter-hour's memory. "Oh, and he was singing naughty chanteys with the whiskery poet fellow."

"Oh." Lady Maudelaine twiddled the fringe on the chair arm. "Well." Seeing that Gwen only stared devotedly at the chubby pootock, she proceeded, as much to herself as not. "I don't know how he can be so carefree. I mean, I know he didn't love her anymore or anything, so he shouldn't be mourning her, but there's bound to be unpleasantness and an investigation. I don't know why the Peace Troops aren't here already. I'd have called daddy, but . . . Well. I mean . . ."

Gwen looked up brightly. "Maybe Lord Roderick's handling it himself. Something about diplomatic immunity? He's awfully clever."

Maudelaine relaxed slightly. "Maybe that's it. But Siphuncle . . . can't be glad she's dead. He can't have done it, now, can he? Or he'd be pretending to mourn her or swearing vengeance at her killer or something. But I didn't see him after breakfast that day, so he didn't see me . . . and I'm worried."

Gwen looked over at Maudelaine vacantly. "Oh, I heard the funniest thing. Svarabakti was a Fausta agent. Isn't that the uttermost utter scream and ho-di-ho-ho? A girl like that couldn't be a cutthroat space pirate. She'd ruin her fingernails."

"Svarabakti?" Lady Maudelaine changed colour and gripped so tightly on the chair arm that some of the fringe came away in her hands. "So that . . . explains it. A traitor to the Empire. To Shard. To my daddy. Maybe I did the right thing after all. Maybe I should be glad I . . ." Maudelaine looked furtively across at Gwen, then lay back in her chair with relief.

Gwen held up Warbert at arm's length, eyeing him fondly. "Oh, you don't suppose the people who made Warbert could make me a dog whale? A big blue one with blue and gold sequins around his eyes? Wouldn't that be adorable?"

"Just adorable," Maudelaine agreed weakly.

30

The air had chilled. A storm threatened. Garamond felt the stone of the tower still warm from earlier sunshine. The stone warmed the back of his head, stone on the outside of the tower.

The sill of the arched window bit into his back below his shoulder blades. Looking up, he could see the eaves of the conical roof of the tower. Under the edges of the tiles, birds had nested. The nests lay empty now. *Why in the blithering, blighty, beastly bedamned do I care about ornithology at a time like this?*

He twisted his chin onto his chest and looked at Siphuncle. Siphuncle held him down on the sill, short beard bristling, eyes blazing, and the graddy skull bound to his brow looking now very sorcerous indeed.

Garamond knew twists and pivots and kicks to be used at such times, but he jolly well didn't want to pivot himself some six or eight floors down into the tarn. Or onto the rocks at its edge.

He relaxed his legs and slumped his lower back, trying to keep all his weight low and on the inside. Siphuncle's eyes looked directly into his.

Feeling Garamond shift under his hands, Siphuncle moved. His expression changed. He grasped Garamond firmly by the shoulders and heaved him up into the center of the tower.

If he plans to eject me in one easy toss, Garamond thought bitterly, *he'll have to think again. I'm too young to—what's the word?—defenestrate*. Garamond put a quick knee where it would do the most good, and as Siphuncle doubled over, brought him face down on the stone floor and sat on his head.

He felt Siphuncle gasp for breath, but held on mercilessly. He faced life or death on the tower top, and the chance of Siphuncle escaping or leaping to doom below.

"I say," Siphuncle gasped when he had the breath to speak. "I say, I've changed my mind. I don't like it up here. You didn't happen to notice that I pulled you back inside?" He employed a tone of full, rich sarcasm. "Once I decided not to do you a damage, couldn't you have let bygones go?"

"You almost killed me," Garamond returned, aggrieved.

"Ah, that's the point of it all. *Almost*. Almost killed you. Sportsmen say 'Close only counts in horseshoes.' Well, it counts in the law courts, too."

"What changed your mind?" Garamond remained suspicious.

"Do you want to know what changed my mind?" Siphuncle asked, his voice muffled on paving stones. "I'll tell you what changed my mind. I don't know who you are or what you're after, but I looked down and saw my hands on your shoulders, and you looking up trying to figure the next move, and a whole panorama of nothing but down. Rocks, tarn, moors, seven floors below. Do you know what I thought?

"I'd been there before. I'd seen it before. The viewpoint of every third-rate villain in every third-rate vid show. I suppose if I'm going to do anything as drastic as murder, I'm sure as sunrise not going to do it in a third-rate way.

"Now," Siphuncle ended, "if you'd get off me and let me get a wash and a clean suit, you can take me to the lock house or whatever you have in mind, but kindly get off my back."

"Oh, frightfully sorry, old chap. Thought you were going to take another swing at me. You're quite sure you're not? It's hardly my practice to go about sitting on chaps when the dust of battle has settled, I assure you. But I want it thoroughly understood you aren't heaving me off the battlements."

"I won't answer for what I'll do if you don't stop making apologetic gestures and get your ruddy, bloody, lead-heavy rearward portions off me."

"Oh, frightfully sorry." Groaning slightly, glaring slightly, the two rose and started down the stairs.

31

Lord Roderick floated in a laudanum-hazy fever dream, a daydream in which he led all his musicians—playing marvelously in key—through the rhapsodic jubilations and tintinnabulations of Commonwealth Day. He didn't open his eyes at the sound of his door unlatching, nor of footsteps crossing his Khaarnwork carpet. He knew that behind his dream lay one dream more: deeper, more fantastic, hideous, in which someone had died. No, worse than died.

He had to keep that death hidden behind an occulting curtain of forgetfulness. If he opened his eyes, he might have to see— something other than flautists and hornblowers enriching Kettle-wharf's heady tropic air with rejoicing.

The daydream could not last. He heard someone drop to kneel at his bedside, hands imploringly touching his shoulder, warm breath on his cheek. His eyelids fluttered up a fraction. Almost face-to-face with him hovered Lady Maudelaine.

"Maudelaine!" he admonished weakly. He should be ecstatic at the thought of a comely blonde throwing herself down at his bedside, but not this afternoon. He didn't fancy Maudelaine as much as he had Svarabakti, but he fancied anyone who would play audience to the drama of his life.

"Oh good! You're awake!" Having made sure of this by firmly grasping his upper arm—fortunately not the arm in a sling—she asked dramatically, "What have you made me do?"

Usher blanched and held his breath.

The governor's daughter elaborated, "Am I going to be the cause of a second Shardé uprising? Will there be blood on the streets on my account? The first time—the Separatist Stylistic Schism—twelve people were killed. Twelve! I couldn't live with that on my conscience. Whatever I am, whatever I've done, I've always been loyal to the Empire."

Fever dreams wafted across Usher's vision. "Have you ever played a lute?" he asked.

"A what? What are you talking about? I'm not one of your musicians, you know. I'm talking about loyalty."

"So am I." Lord Roderick pulled himself together with dignity. "Do you think I would plan music and dance for Commonwealth Day if I were not loyal? Do you think I would hold such a house party with such elaborate practicing if I expected—or wanted—a Separatist uprising? Some have criticized my fripperies and fopperies, but they have always been those of a Loyalist."

Maudelaine wavered. She had a number of questions yet to ask, but she realized many things were better left unsaid. If she were overheard, if Usher, in his fever, were to repeat her words, the results could be disastrous. She was used to getting what she wanted by the simple expedient of asking for it *now*. She had to have answers, but after a moment of internal struggle, she realized she dare not ask further today. "Oh, *I* see. It sounds clear enough if you put it that way. Thank you."

She left Roderick to his dreaming, and directly outside his door fell into Gaust Kennes' arms.

This was no coincidence. For months he had dogged her path. Now, though, as Venga Avest, he followed and watched over her from a loftier plane. Kennes had wanted desperately to be near her. The Venga Avest merely wanted to oversee her welfare. He had waited for her with the detached calm of a spiritual advisor. Thus it was that when she left Usher's room and tripped over the toe of Kennes' boot, it was she who grasped him for support.

He caught her and held her upright. He had never before been closer to her than when they clasped hands at breakfast. This was an intoxicating encounter, but the Venga Avest could better stand the heady moment than could the governor's agent.

Maudelaine clung to him, her head on his black-clad shoulder. She shuddered.

"There now, you're overwrought. Let us go in here." He led the way into the secluded octagonal room where Gwen had found the bristlefish. Not being in an investigative mood, he found no skeleton nor did he think of murder nor of Svarabakti, living or dead, for quite some satisfactory time.

Gwen and Garamond returned to the Red Death Tapestry Room to rest and regroup. Coming up passages at right angles to each other, they cannoned off one another outside their door. Getting their breaths back, they began speaking at once.

"If I ever see another toy pootock—"

"What ails Siphuncle, I'd like to know?"

"The girl is so spoiled, so self-centered—"

"Do you know what I think he did—?"

Garamond recovered first, bowed extravagantly for Gwen to precede him into the room, and, once inside, stood with his back against the door, grimacing slightly as he tried to get various twists out of his spine.

Gwen threw herself upon his breast, causing him to wince, and pretended to sob out her troubles. "I interviewed Lady Maudelaine all right. Nothing between her ears whatsoever. She'd tell anything to a sympathetic listener. Anything. I had to pretend to be even denser than she is, and that was a challenge. I swear, I started nearly every sentence with, 'Oh!' I got frightened toward the end that if I said 'Oh!' once more, something would snap and I'd be paralyzed with a permanently circular mouth, like a hoots fish. She ended by saying she might have done the right thing after all, that maybe she should be glad. She stopped there, but presumably glad for what she did. But did she . . . ? Garamond, what's the matter?"

"Why," Garamond asked with a set and artificial grin to his face, "do you think anything's wrong?"

"Because you're wriggling and twitching as if you had a spider in your trousies, and your face looks like Dao Dyen Huye's *Scroll of Twelve Anguishes*."

"Dao Dyen Huye the Elder," Garamond corrected. "My back's a bit out of order from lying over the upper windowsill of one of the lower towers. Siphuncle and I argued all the way down the stairs whether it was seven or eight floors high. Seeing that both the entry hall and the library are twice as lofty as the ordinary rooms of that wing—"

"What were you doing lying over the windowsill?"

"Trying to get back in. I know. You're going to ask, why was I about to fall out? Because Siphuncle, in his efforts to convince me that he is neither a jealous nor a violent man, tried to push me."

"Then how . . . ?" Gwen held her cousin rather more tightly than usual, realized its effect on his back, and released her hold a fraction.

"Because Siphuncle changed his mind. He's waiting to see if he's going to be locked up first for attempted murder or the other kind."

"Well, we can't do what we planned to do if your back's in a double half hitch. Take off your tunic, lie face down on the bed—"

"No, really, I'll be all right," Garamond protested.

A few moments later, Borcubast, silent footed, entered as previously arranged, to find Gwen, on the bed, sitting in the middle of her cousin's bare back, apparently throttling the life out of him. This vignette took on an even more macabre air played out against the backdrop of a vast, sombre tapestry portraying Prince Prospero falling lifeless before the Spectre of the Red Death.

"Pardon me," Borcubast announced firmly, "but ye was askin' about Yotu, and now that yer in, I'm tellin' ye."

Gwen turned to say, "Thank you. Just a minute," over her shoulder, gave Garamond the type of twisting wrench with which the undercook professionally dispatched geese for the oven, and rose to welcome the rather confused butler.

To his relief, Garamond rose also, shook himself so several vertebrae popped audibly into place, sighed utter contentment, and resumed his tunic. "Speak, O Borcubast. I would hear thy discourse."

"Don't know about a discus in this house, though I had a fair hand at the toss in my day, both for the sport of it and the beheading of Franji. But as for Yotu"—he brought his heels together in the sketch of a salute, leaving his bowed knees some distance from one another—"that Yotu! He went to the Scroll Room, as ye warned me, but I had two maids and a footman making a dust and a bother, and told him he'd have to come back later, as his lordship had ordered some cleaning and rearranging. At the word rearranging, his face changed, but whether for the better or worse I'd be hard put to say.

"To cut my words short, he didn't get into the Scroll Room, and he didn't get into some other rooms where he 'thought he'd left something.' Not Svarabakti's suite, nor Siphuncle's, nor the master's dressing room, as has a door from the hall that I had the bootboy watching. Though it's not boots he does, but anything the rest of us is too large or slow for doing, but the master's a great one for tradition, so Boots he's called.

"Now, I didn't let on as if I knowed he was after something as he shouldn't, and he didn't trouble me with argyments and bribifyin', but his face gets lower and lower as the mornin' passes, and his cheek tufts is quiverin' like sedges in a hurrycane. Speakin' whereupon, I called up the weather department and asked after that storm, and they said they'd have it to order, but perhaps an hour late, nothing being perfect under the Daystar.

"Meanin'"—Borcubast contrived to look solemn—"ye'll have time for a bite of luncheon and a bit of a rest or a look around before ye get set on that playactin' ye've mentioned."

Gwen and Garamond nodded and made shushing motions.

"I know. Never a word. When there's murder done, no matter how deserved, there's retrybution, and I won't say the Empire's way of it is worse than our old way as we had back home. Spilled blood's worse nor spilled water, even on the Cold Desert, though for a lady with a knife in her buzzum, she hadn't much blood to speak of."

"Ah, you noticed that too?" Gwen leaned close to the old Kulmar. "You've good eyes and a good head. You may have used them in odd ways over the last days." The old man backed away a step. "But if you say nothing of these things, it can't be the worse for you."

"Right," Garamond seconded. "Now, how about a speck of lunch?"

32

"I won't say this is going to work without a hitch"—
Garamond, fussing with the internals of his blaster, turned to
Gwen in a state of high confidence—"but I can't think of any-
thing we've forgotten."

Gwen, of warier mould, made no answer. She had made her
preparations, and had double-checked Garamond's. The two, re-
plete with cheese dumplings, had repaired to their room, watched
over by the tapestried Spectre of Red Death, to check their notes.
They were so checking, on the display plate of Garamond's vambrace, when Kennes entered.

"Ah, Kennes," Gwen smiled with genuine warmth. After all,
matters had begun to fall into place, and Kennes was the first of
them. "We were expecting you."

Though shaken at this statement, Kennes recovered quickly. "I
just dropped up here to offer my help," he remarked in a tone
rather like his ordinary one, but with the added authority of a man
who has spent several days as a Venga Avest. "If we don't have
this case sewed up and in the governor's hands at dawn, it won't
be a missing parchment and a dead singer alone we have to deal
with, but Inspector General Carp as well." He made it evident
that Inspector General Carp outclassed mere sensitive documents
and mysterious corpses as a first-class nuisance.

"Very kind offer, Kennes, old chap." Garamond switched off
the display on his vambrace in a let's-get-down-to-business fashion. And to prevent Kennes peeking. "What did you have in
mind?"

"Oh." Kennes sat back in a carved wooden chair like a throne,
an appropriate seat for a Venga Avest. "I had a talk with three
charming young people: Kelesophos, Patrice, and Hyota-ya.
They knew of an interesting connection between the Separatists
and the Fausta. Not that they knew what they were telling me.
Perhaps you'd like to hear about it."

"We'd be glad to," Gwen said blithely, "if I hadn't known it all before I even entered the mansion."

Garamond asked, "Do you know if it relates to the murder?"

Austerely, steepling his fingers and examining the carved ceiling beams with interest, Kennes dropped what he hoped to be a bombshell. "I know how it relates to the document. A most insolent piece of treason, intended—"

"Intended," Gwen took up the thread, "to net the Fausta a navy light cruiser or two, good for better than average piracy and an independent Shardworld to share in the spoils."

Kennes smiled benevolently. "You two are a clever couple of sleuths. I haven't a clue how you do it. Consider the murder—I have yet to discover whether it's a crime of passion or a crime of politics. Do you know?"

"We have an idea." Garamond beamed his satisfaction. To be called clever by Kennes warmed his very marrow. And only this morning he had worried that he might be a bit dense. "We could let you glance over a list of clues, if you'd . . . oh, I don't know."

Kennes sat in suspense. If only he could avoid a few unpleasant issues and reach the governor with the problems solved and the credit all to himself. . . . And here the Grays sat ready to give clues away.

"If, perhaps"—Garamond, having holstered his blaster, blandly polished his fingertips on one of the embroidered handkerchees Lord Roderick supplied for his guests. "If perhaps you'd care to tell us how you breached our security system to leave a bomb in our office and delay our departure."

"So you guessed I did that? You noticed the little fantasy touch of the word 'nevermore' in antique script? I practiced for an hour on that alone."

"Once we listened to the tapes of that peculiar literature Lord R. fancies," Gwen elucidated, "we had no doubt of the meaning or the perpetrator. But how did you get in?"

Kennes examined his steepled fingers with mild interest, gave an experimental twiddle to his thumbs, and explained innocently, "I simply went to the Peace Office with proper authorizations from the governor, asked to examine your office to complete your security clearance before employing you in an official capacity, and reminded them to switch off your security system when they got my signal. Not precisely legal, but the governor carries a weight in his province beyond the haggles and niggles of the finer points of law."

"Very neat use of the materials at hand," Gwen congratulated, "if I may speak so of the governor. The clues?" She gestured sweepingly to Garamond who produced a roll of parchment—ordinary vegetable parchment, but still impressive in an Empire that tended to make obeisance to Documents, particularly those with numerous seals and ribbons.

Through Borcubast's good offices, Garamond had obtained a plentiful supply of sealing wax. Using his and Gwen's personal seals (mere affectations in a legal light, though that light would never shine on this paper), some old coins in Usher's collection, Gwen's opal ring, and the engraved handle of a spoon, Garamond had made a number of interesting impressions. A number of ribbons donated from one of Patrice's hats set the finishing touch.

Gwen set out a small table, and Kennes unrolled the scroll on it portentously. "Amusing," he muttered, recognizing the sources of some of the seals. "Rather good penmanship for these days . . . Yours, Garamond?"

Garamond nodded, waiting as Kennes read.

"Why you!" The explosion came. "Why you unprincipled pair of wharf lizards! It's just a game. One of those puzzle lists such as the antique mystery-mongers made. You might find a dozen like this among the odd books Usher fancies."

"We did," Gwen said simply.

"But these are real clues?" Kennes looked at the Grays sidelong. "They have significance?"

"Oh, yes. We're rather proud of them. Read them out." The two sat back to listen with unalloyed pleasure to the fruits of their labours.

Tentatively, as if he expected to be the butt of a joke, Kennes read:

"The parchment means more to the Separatists complete.
It means more to the Loyalists destroyed.
Yotu is a Separatist.
Hyota-ya is a Loyalist.
Lady Maudelaine acts inconsistently.
Lady Svarabakti acted consistently.
Lord Roderick has a bandage on his head and a sling on his arm.
Where the stone fell upon him, a webwire was found.
Lord Roderick has remarkably sensitive nerves.
He invites rowdy guests and keeps noisy pootocks.

Fish bones appeared in a chest, wooden.
A fish knife appeared in a chest, Svarabakti's."

Kennes looked up, his raised eyebrow daring his listeners to break into peals of laughter at his discomfiture. "You're sure Yotu is a Separatist?" he asked at last.

"He certainly doesn't mind people thinking so," Garamond said with feeling.

Kennes glared back at the list. His puzzlement was almost palpable. "Some of these entries are self-evident; some are insignificant. Precisely like the lists in antique mysteries. Minds today are trained above such things," he evaded loftily. "I could no more solve the case from this list than from a conundrum or a crossword puzzle. However, I will take it with me if I may. It may be of use in evidence." Not adding, *evidence of your incompetence, irrelevance, and insanity,* as he rather wished to say, Kennes rose and departed.

Moments later the man-high Ostrey-Edvil bronze bell in the topmost tower, the bell that called Lord Roderick's guests to supper or to chapel, tolled ominously.

Knowing this was neither the time to sup nor to pray, guests poked heads out of doors and gathered on landings; curious, excited, worried, frightened.

"Is there a fire?"

"Has someone else been killed?"

"Is Lord Roderick all right?"

"Where are we to go?"

"Has anyone seen my wife?"

"Has anyone seen my diamonds?"

Questions whirled in a storm around the waiting servants, and in answer, a deafening crack of thunder split the firmament overhead and echoed, earthquakelike, across the tarn and moors.

In the following silence, servants herded guests into the great hall, where seats around a roaring fireplace, hot cyder, and an atmosphere of anticipation held the attention of all.

Outdoors, rain fell with the sound and force of hail.

33

When all the guests and most of the servants had assembled, Borcubast signalled to a pair of footmen. The air of suspense, heightened not only by the weather and hot cyder but also by a mood that the room itself took on, reached such a pitch that the guests would not have been surprised by the appearance of the Empress, a fifty-foot Willowwall dragon lizard, or a troupe of performing graddies in caps and bells. Even the Spectre of the Red Death, a pit and a pendulum, or a homicidal orangutan might have been taken in stride.

With only mild and polite enthusiasm, the guests greeted the entry of Lord Roderick, pale and drawn, leaning on two footmen. They helped him onto a sofa near the fire, and Lady Maudelaine ran up busily to plump a heap of cushions for him to recline upon as was his wont.

Thunder muttered its accompaniment to his entry, and the lightning that flashed outside the high and narrow windows only served to highlight the linen bandage and sling, the stigmata of his injury.

"You may wonder why I have gathered you together," Usher began in a voice little stronger than a whisper. The guests leaned closer. Someone surged forward between the seats.

Garamond now stood over his host, his cloak swirling in a most picturesque manner. He brandished a blaster at the vaulted ceiling and mouthed soundlessly as an Olympian thunder roll shook the very foundations of the manor.

Cocking an exasperated eyebrow at the sky, Garamond began again.

"I was saying, Lord Roderick called you together"—he essayed a rascally sneer—"because I made him do it."

Gwen, standing near the door to the main stairway, drew breath and prayed within herself, *I hope he gets this part right.*

"Loose words have been used in this house," Garamond continued, dusting his blaster barrel unnecessarily with a lace handkerchee, "about the scoundrelly, stick-at-naught rogues of the spaceways, the intrepid, indeefatoogable . . ." Gwen held her head in her hands. "The men and women ready to fly into hell and stoke up its furnaces if they hoped to find loot in the process, the Fausta."

Against intention, both theirs and Garamond's, the crowd cheered enthusiastically. It took some time of frowning, stomping about in large, piratical boots he had gotten, of all places, from the bootboy, and brandishing his blaster for Garamond to quiet them.

"Some of you here know more about the Fausta than it's healthy to know, and some of you have told more about them than it's healthy to tell."

Gwen, stationed where she could see the faces of most of the crowd, noted that, as she feared, nearly everyone looked guilty and peculiar, giving no additional clues.

"I came here"—Garamond gave a hearty stomp with his boot heel to indicate where *here* was, and winced at the reminder that the boots were a size too small—"unexpected, unannounced, uninvited, for one reason: to find the traitor in our midst and recover the secret document that traitor stole."

Someone—could it have been Dheloris?—corrected, "That's two reasons."

It must have been Dheloris. Fettle overruled cuttingly, *"Those* are two reasons."

"The traitor and the secret document," Garamond reminded. "Both are within this house." Thunder rumbled hearty applause. "I am here to unmask the traitor and disclose his traitory. His traitorhood. Blast it, what's come over my tongue?"

"Stage fright?" Lady Maudelaine asked helpfully.

"Tongue longer than his vocabulary," Yotu whispered to Yin.

"Treachery. You mean treachery," Fettle assisted.

"I say," asked Siphuncle, who had—in the tower with Garamond sitting on his head—given up guessing which side Garamond was on, "do you mean treachery against the Empire or treachery against the Fausta?"

Garamond stamped and winced once more. "I mean treachery foul and simple. One among you removed a document"—Lady Maudelaine bounced righteously in her chair—"of enormous value to both the Fausta, the Empire, and the Shardé Separatists."

"That's not *both,"* Dheloris interjected. *"Those,"* she had learned her lesson, "are three competitors."

"This," Garamond said sternly, "is the preliminary hearing upon a traitor in the house of an Imperial ambassador. Because of the setting, diplomatic immunity allows a freedom of procedure impossible in law courts of the Empire. This is a species of trial for a crime for which the punishment among the Fausta is death and disfiguration, and in the Empire . . . the punishment fits the crime. This, fatted guests of an effete noble, is a trial. What did you think it was, a grammar lesson?"

Thunder rumbled grudging agreement. In an unexpected silence, Lord Roderick could be heard to mutter, "I would have said it was improvisational theater."

"Even at this moment," Garamond said firmly, striding up and down in front of the fire, "three of my operatives are searching the guest rooms for incriminating evidence."

In an irresistible wave, the guests rose. They hurried toward their rooms as best they could in spite of collisions with one another, the stepping on of feet, and loud cries, none of which were complimentary to Garamond.

"However," Garamond bellowed, bringing them to a standstill, "I have here a particular document of considerable interest." From under his cloak, he waved a roll of purple parchment. The footmen took this opportunity to block the exits of the room, and the guests, attracted by the thought of a secret document, subsided, with many a grunt and shuffle, to find out as much as they could of what they shouldn't.

Garamond unrolled the scroll. The atmosphere became almost unbearably electric with anticipation.

Yotu, ruddy scales and whiskers a-bristle, and Kennes, in the sober demeanor of Venga Avest, rose to protest.

"You can't read that!" Yotu shrieked. Kennes intoned the same words. The two looked furiously at one another.

"That cannot be read," Kennes pronounced somberly, throwing out a hand to point dramatically at the offending parchment. "I forbid you, in the name of the governor, to read a word of that document."

Lord Roderick nodded agreement.

"You speak for the governor?" Garamond challenged.

"I do."

Yotu leaped up and down with rage and frustration. "What of the governor? What of the Empire? I say you would not dare read that for the shame and trembling of the parliament. Give it me, and I will send it to that water cow who sits the Oriel-Moss-marching throne. May she never bear another calf!"

"Oh, I say!" the guests chorused.

"Rather blunt language, that."

"Don't know where you are with these backworld provincials."

"Shameful thing to call Her Puissant Majesty."

"Oh, I don't know. Last time I saw her she looked a bit like a water cow. I mean the big brown eyes, of course. Silly jest. Meant nothing by it."

"Give it me!" Yotu continued to bounce up and down, his tail, vest tassles, and the baggy bottoms of his Turkish trousers, half a cycle behind, bounced down and up. With a desperate spring, he wrenched the scroll from Garamond's hand, fled to the other end of the room, and found the doors blocked against him. Defiantly he unrolled the document and prepared to read it openly himself rather than have it destroyed. He glanced, gaped, and threw it from him contemptuously.

Fettle snatched it up and stood staring at it, puzzled. "I do say, if this is a secret document, I should like to know why. Roderick, I'd think you would be proud to have this read aloud here in your hall and in the presence of your friends."

Lord Roderick responded straightforwardly by putting his head under one of his cushions.

"Well!" Fettle cleared his throat in an after-dinner-speaking manner. "Our host may be overcome with momentary modesty, but I am sure all of you are waiting to hear what is said in this momentous document." He was correct. Many would have committed violence from sheer curiosity. "It says here, 'Whereas it has come to the attention of the Shardé Native Chief that Lord Roderick Usher has caused to be built a red stripe-stone monumental fountain honoring those who labour in the fields of Shard, shaped in the likeness of a Shardé farm lad pouring forth the plenteous waters of our land upon a whitefruit sprout from an old oaken bucket, we hereby decree that this fountain, free to the use of all, shall be known as the Usher Gusher.'"

The audience tittered and Lord Roderick groaned.

Yotu leaped onto a chair. "That was the wrong scroll!" he shouted in disgust. "The wrong scroll, and with the inferior and debased calligraphy of a hired scribe. I am appalled that anyone could consider it of any importance whatsoever." He made as if to stalk in a dudgeon from the hall. Footmen turned him back with the utmost courtesy.

"There," Garamond said and spread the wings of his cloak glossy black before the fire as if at a wish he would vanish in smoke up the chimney. "I think we've proved who our traitor is, one who has pride in his tr . . . treachery. You have seen Yotu, and you can testify to what he has said, and that's that."

Garamond glanced at his vambrace, adjusted the display plate, and remarked offhandedly, "I'm surprised anyone thought I'd bring a valuable document before such a volatile crew. It's in a safe place and will be in the governor's hands by dawn. Once he's seen it, he'll destroy it.

"After all, it's a silly, stupid thing. The Shardé Native Chief wrote it while in his cups, and much may be forgiven when something is written under the influence of plum brandy. Likely, he would have burnt it in the morning if Yotu hadn't brought it away to the governor. While the governor was still wondering what to do, Yotu must have whispered many things in many ears."

Siphuncle stood. "You've hinted and suggested and implied here for half an hour, but who under Daystar are you? You're no Fausta agent if you're complaining about treachery to the Empire, much less a Separatist. And will you jolly well tell us what's in that letter, or tell us for once and for all that we won't ever hear it?"

"Oh, I'm just a loyal Imperial citizen doing my duty," Garamond said modestly.

"And showing off." Lady Maudelaine, bitter, would have preferred center stage. Next she remembered that Garamond knew a number of things about her that she didn't need publicized, and shut her mouth with a pout.

"As for the letter," Garamond resumed, "it's so childish that it would never have caused an interplanetary incident if it hadn't been written on the eve of Shardworld entering the Imperial Commonwealth. It's only the sort of thing naughty children write on walls, not that the Shardé Native Chief is a naughty boy, but plum brandy is potent tipple.

"In the midst of unwise remarks about Imperial oppression and the unfairness of setting up humans to govern Shard, as if he'd forgotten fully half the provincial governors are Shardé and that the chief himself can overrule any governor, he said—" Garamond glanced at the display plate of his vambrace again, upped the magnification, and blushed—"in his letter, the chief called Her Imperial Majesty a pimple-rumped biscuit face. Or vice versa."

The guests, noble and celebrities of a number of worlds, laughed and stomped with the abandon of rustics at a vegetable fair.

34

Rain gusted heavily against the windows facing the tarn, and the mood in the great hall turned to one of urgent questing and apprehension. For a moment Gwen felt as if there might have been something to what Yin had said about spirits. The shadows of voices, like those of an enormous crowd so distant as to be at the very limit of hearing, seemed to whisper insistently that something must be shown or said or done. She felt a gnawing frustration that she didn't know what the spirit voices wanted.

She shook herself, and the certainty that she had heard anything at all passed off. It might have been any trick of the mind, like the impression of voices heard in running water, in the static of an untuned vid, or the whine of any machine.

Looking around her, though, Gwen knew that most of the guests and a few of the Kulmar servants had heard what she had heard. The Shardé, apparently sensitive to this phenomenon, fidgeted and cocked their jug ears feverishly. Beads of sweat dewed Lord Roderick's brow as he lay twisting uneasily upon his couch.

Thunder rattled the slates and the plates, and Kelesophos, Patrice, and Hyota-ya entered at the door from the stairs where Gwen had been waiting for them.

"Have you found anything?" she asked.

Hyota-ya, spokesman of the moment, shook his head between hunched shoulders and ran nervous fingers over his ears as if to rid them of the whispers. "Tapes and discs enough to prove Yotu's guilt. Nothing to show against Yin—other than what Mr. Gray heard. And nothing at all to show that anyone but Svarabakti had dealings with the Fausta. But of course, if people were careful not to keep things, or hid them better than Miss Svarabakti did, we wouldn't know."

"Well, you did your best, and more," Gwen congratulated. "Yotu is all but imprisoned, and a Loyalist should be glad to have helped in that. Here, stand by. Things might get a bit sticky."

Garamond stood tall on the hearthstone, no longer posturing

and posing. Not even Dheloris would have thought now to correct his grammar or make fun of his eccentricities.

Outside, dusk deepened, but a curious glow wavered around the window rims. Some of the guests pointed and whispered, and some made signs of warding from superstitions they would normally have been ashamed to admit they knew.

Lord Roderick raised himself upon the cushions. Garamond turned to him. Usher gestured briefly to the ghost-light glow. "It is nothing. A natural phenomenon. In electric weather, in times of storm, the peculiar growths of fungus that web my home tend to glow with that cold, wavering luminosity. I have oft thought to have a natural philosopher analyze the growths, such as I have seen nowhere else, and perhaps I shall do so in time. I have always assumed they had the same cold light as blink flies and lantern beetles, and the sea lights that make fire-foam at the prows of ships. It is nothing to fear."

Garamond, finding an opening, solemnly put his fingertips to his brow. "No, we need not fear the ghostly lights and the fury of the storm so much as the storms within ourselves. The cold lights hurt no one; we have Lord Roderick's word. But the warm hand of someone under this roof struck down Svarabakti. Who has done it?"

The half-guessed whispers of the spirit of the house urgently echoed the question.

"Now Yotu"—Garamond pointed him out with an eloquent gesture—"Yotu is traitor to the Empire, and so—as some of you know—was Svarabakti. As unlikely as it may seem, she was a Fausta agent. She had a tape ready to mail to Che Chenander, an alias of a known agent of the Fausta. It's only a *poste restante* address, so it's not likely we'll learn anything from that—Chenander's a careful one. We'll probably never know why Svarabakti joined the cause. It may have been at the urging of a friend of hers, Georgios, the notorious Fausta pilot.

"She knew where the parchment was that Yotu wanted to use for the advantage of the Separatists, and though his use of it would have benefited the Fausta, she might have wanted it in her own hands.

"She could have threatened, blackmailed—"

Yotu leaped onto his chair again. "You lie!" he screamed shrilly, his cheek tufts bristling. "You lie!"

"What a mercy that's over," Gwen said under her breath.

"What are you saying?" Hyota-ya had heard her and, puzzled, turned his large trusting eyes to hers.

"What I meant was," Gwen observed in an undertone, "in any confrontation like this, someone always shouts, 'You lie!' It's so embarrassingly unoriginal, but at least it's behind us for tonight."

"Ah!" Hyota-ya turned away, still puzzled.

Siphuncle stood. "I don't know what it means, but Onesday night Svarabakti said some uncomplimentary things about Fausta's ability to organize."

"That may be"—Garamond nodded briefly—"but likely that was only camouflage. She was one of the Fausta all right.

"And Yotu, as a Separatist traitor, would be the most likely murderer, if he had not been committing a different crime that morning."

Yotu stamped his bare feet, huffing and snorting.

"Yes, as you were practicing the revelry that would celebrate Shard's entry into the Commonwealth, Yotu wished for no such thing. Yotu, garbed in festive black and scarlet like all his fellow revelers, was dancing galliards, galops, and gallivants on the green, and playing a three-string fiddle most excruciatingly out of tune."

"Well!" Yotu said firmly, proud he had at least struck a sour note for Separatism. He fluffed out his russet scales and sat down with finality.

"With him too, Yin danced and frolicked, innocent—at least of murder."

Yin lowered her eyelids haughtily.

"Yin and Yotu were not close to Svarabakti except politically. Murder is more common in the household than between strangers. We often hurt the ones we once loved. Still, there are exceptions. Some have noticed that Dheloris and Fettle have behaved oddly since the murder. We ask, what connection might they have to Svarabakti?"

Dheloris quivered all over in a curious fashion, as if an electric current were being run through a gelatinous mass.

Fettle protruded his chin whiskers menacingly. "Me! What about Siphuncle? Now that's the man with a grudge against the once-dear departed."

"I say," Siphuncle protested. "Here the two of us were composing chanteys this breakfast, and now you want to turn me over to the hangman. Is there no honor among artists?"

"Not if you did it and we didn't," Dheloris snapped, her topmost chin in the air.

"Could Svarabakti"—Garamond raised his voice and restored momentary order—"have known a guilty secret about these two that they, or one of them, would have killed to protect?"

The two edged their chairs slightly from each other.

"They do have a secret," Garamond admitted, "and—" Dheloris surged to her feet, lowered her head, and charged.

Gwen whispered to Patrice, "I never knew so large a woman could move so fast."

"Oh, it's all a matter of muscle tone. I've known dancers who lost their figures but not their musculature and remained quite light on their feet."

The blond virago seemed determined to give Garamond the drubbing she usually reserved for flatstone drums. She clutched at him, an avalanche in black velvet, tiny pink hands absurdly menacing, eyes narrowed under pale, inconspicuous brows.

As she did so, Lord Roderick shifted slightly on his couch and extended a slippered foot, tripping the ample amazon.

Garamond rose from the hearth rug, disentangled himself from Dheloris, and discreetly thanked Lord Roderick.

"Now, madam," Garamond said sternly, helping to heave her to her feet, "you mustn't go on like this. It could ruin your reputation far worse than the disclosure of any secret except murder. There, back to your seat."

Seething, she went, and thunder applauded her exit.

"No, Dheloris and Fettle weren't a-dancing on the green that morning, but neither were they a-murdering. Fettle was in his room, quarreling with his wife . . ." A number of indrawn breaths registered shock and surprise. ". . . And overheard by the bootboy. This same boy overheard Dheloris, in her room, arguing with her husband." The chorus of shocked gasps echoed louder. "In fact, Dheloris and her husband, Fettle . . ."

The guests, with no further lung space for gasps, gaped in silence. The fire crackled in the lull, rain and wind beat furiously upon the windows, shadows moved stealthily in the corners, and the ghost-light wavered through the coloured glass of the high windows. The sense of urgent entreaty surged in waves throughout the room.

"Dheloris and her husband, Fettle," Garamond repeated, "were arguing as to whether they should publicly reveal their marriage. Apparently Dheloris' father forbids her to throw away her reputation of musical genius by allying with, I quote, 'a lewd hedgehog whose only attainment is the dubious ability to rhyme words with less than five letters.'"

Fettle struggled in the quandary of whether to vent his anger first on Garamond or the bootboy.

"Whereas Fettle's mother has no intention of giving over her clever darling to, and I do not quote"—Garamond thus halted the lady in another furious charge—"Dheloris. The two seem somewhat financially dependent upon their parents, but, if I might suggest that the two of you introduce your respective parents to one another, they might find many views in common and bless your union. On the other hand, they may not."

Garamond cleared his throat, turned, and bowed to Lady Maudelaine. She did not return the courtesy. "Now I come," he continued, "to those with a closer interest in Svarabakti's welfare —or otherwise. Lady Maudelaine and Svarabakti, as you may have heard in their own words yesterday at breakfast, were rivals. Svarabakti struck Lady Maudelaine in the face. The scars, though healing, still show. Slower to heal are blows to the heart. We all saw Lady Maudelaine threaten Svarabakti with a fish knife."

Lady Maudelaine looked down her nose at the entire assembly, not deigning to protest at this point.

"Later that day, the knife, or one identical to it, found its way into Svarabakti's heart. The lady may be excused for using the knife at breakfast to prevent further violence. But think how Svarabakti's public humiliation of the girl may have festered in her until Lady Maudelaine saw her rival again.

"We know, through an observant serving maid, Marli, that the knife was not visible in Lady Maudelaine's room after she left the buffet. However, it may have been concealed. When I discovered the body in the chapel, it showed no signs of a struggle such as there should have been if the two women, of apparently equal strength, fought. The corpse wore a garnet necklace belonging to Lady Maudelaine. That lady would probably have taken it away if she had killed the singer, but then again, she might have been interrupted.

"The strongest point in Lady Maudelaine's defense is that the corpse had been artifically laid out on the altar. It would have been very difficult for Lady Maudelaine to lift the somewhat larger and heavier woman to that height. But not impossible. For the moment Lady Maudelaine's guilt or innocence is uncertain.

"We move on to Siphuncle, wronged, as Fettle has reminded

us, by the woman who at one time professed to love him, who had thrown him over, but who was still jealous of Lady Maudelaine's attentions to him. Not only was he wronged by her, but he saw her strike the lady who had become his friend. Directly after they left the breakfast room, Siphuncle and Svarabakti quarreled violently and threatened death to one another, again overheard.

"In this case, though, the servant who heard them was in the room with them. If either of them had really intended murder, he or she would have chosen words more carefully. We know how frequently people say, 'I'll kill him,' or even, 'I'll kill you,' and nothing is thought of the matter unless the threatened person dies violently. It's unlikely Siphuncle planned murder at the time he uttered those threats.

"He, like Lady Maudelaine, had a chance to do violence but restrained himself. This speaks for his innocence but doesn't prove it. Neither he nor Lady Maudelaine can be cleared at this point. Who will speak up to clear them?"

The sentient presence of the house echoed, "Who?"

The little kitchen maid hid her face in her apron and sobbed.

"It would be the depth of discourtesy," Garamond resumed, "to suggest that our host had committed murder."

Lord Roderick collapsed farther into his cushions and wiped his brow.

"Still," Garamond argued, "it would be equally discourteous to refrain from mentioning the reasons to presume his innocence. During the essential time yesterday morning, the serving maid Marli and her friend the footman Brennu, worked scrubbing stains in the hall outside Lord Roderick's room. They never saw or heard him leave the room, and as they worked, they heard him move or groan from time to time.

"Although it has been suggested"—Garamond did not meet Gwen's eyes—"that our host is not as ill or seriously injured as it would seem, even if he were in full health, how could he murder a woman in the chapel at the other end of the house when witnesses heard him in his room and didn't see him leave it?"

The guests sighed their relief.

"I have now come to the end of the list of those guests who were inside the house at the time of the murder."

Kennes tried to avoid reminding Garamond otherwise.

"Who could have done this thing? If not the guests, only the servants. The loyal retainers upon whom Lord Roderick depends for comfort, safety, and properly coddled eggs. Can one of these have done the dirty deed?"

The little kitchen maid plied her hankie earnestly, holding tightly with her free hand to one of Borcubast's.

"Can the culprit be—the butler? In the history of crime detection, two mottoes have provided valuable advice throughout the ages; *'cherchez la femme'* and 'the butler dunnit.' The butler keeps all the keys and knows all the secrets. He is omniscient and omnipresent. At times, thinking himself insufficiently rewarded for his labours, he seeks to augment his income. Perhaps he allows his master or the guests of the house to pay him for the courtesy of neglecting to mention certain unsavoury matters. Can Borcubast have acted so?"

Borcubast drew himself up to the full extent allowed by his bandy legs and bowed back. He lifted his large, pendulous nose on high, and looked down it with all the dignity he could muster.

The kitchen maid emitted a number of feeble squeaks until the cook grasped her firmly but gently by the shoulders and gave her a quelling look such as only a woman of Kulmar warrior stock can give.

"But," said Garamond with a flourish, "the butler of the house was with me when I discovered the body. Not only was he with me then, but he had been with me for some time. For quite a long time, showing me all, *all* the glories, beauties, and grotesqueries of the Usher mansion. Nor could he have done the murder before he took me on this tour, because the body, when I found it, was still warm. Borcubast is cleared.

"I believe," Garamond said ironically, "the kitchen maid has something to say."

"Oh, save me! I did it! Oh, save me!" The kitchen maid threw herself at Borcubast's feet.

The old butler stooped, raised her, and kept an arm protectively around her while he said, "There, now, tell what it is ye did. Ye'll never rest easy, nor will any of us below stairs get a wink until ye've told what's done."

"Oh, thank you, Borcubast, sir. Ye won't let them hurt me? Ye've been so kind to a poor, mixy-minded kitchen maid. Don't desert me now. What I did, Mr. Borcubast, sir, was so terrible bad, I don't know what his lordship will do. What I did, sir"— this in response to a hearty nudge in the ribs from the concerned but curious butler—"what I did was I brought his lordship the wrong breakfast."

The chuckles from her audience sent the maid into a fit of blushes and hiccoughs as she twisted and knotted her fingers in an agony of embarrassment and the self-importance of a speaker before the public eye.

"What his lordship ordered," the maid resumed, "was lumpfruit nectar, white wafers, and a coddled goose egg. But ye see, when I were a-settin his tray, my sister Marli a-told me what cook told her about the ladies a-skirmishin' over the buffet. I was that excited and flummoxed in the head by such tales of soap-operafication, as I fixed up the tray with lumpfruit nectar, white wafers, a coddled goose egg, and, oh, help me, sir, and a big kipper of bristlefish."

The guests tittered unabashedly.

"But what I did then, when I was at his lordship's door, and I looks down at the tray and sees that bristlefish and the knife as goes with it . . . What I did then is past telling." She gave herself wholly up to her emotions and sobbed on Borcubast's shoulder while he blushed and patted her back with increasing warmth.

"Then, miss," Garamond suggested, "what if I tell you what I think . . . I mean, what my cousin thinks you did, and you tell us if it's so. My cousin Gwen found the skeleton—" Everyone gasped as gratifyingly as Garamond could wish. "—of a bristlefish in an old chest across the hall from Lord Roderick's room. A rather fresh skeleton. Gwen suggests that, overcome with shock at the realization that you had brought the wrong breakfast, you felt faint and weak, and stumbled into the octagonal room across the hall to sit on the old trunk and rest. To recover your strength, you ate the fish, and to hide the evidence of such a crime as to eat your breakfast outside the kitchen, you put the bones in the trunk. Is this what happened?"

The maid nodded gratefully.

"Then," Garamond warned, "you have seen proof of the maxim, 'crime doth not pay,' and the other, 'lo, thy sins shall find thee out.'"

Garamond looked gravely around the room. "Who else is left? I have dealt with the guests. I have dealt with the servants. But someone here is neither guest nor servant. Rise, Your Excellency, the Venga Avest of Corbo."

Kennes walked up to the hearth, took a central position, and might even have been seen elbowing Garamond slightly to get it. "Lords, ladies, my friends, children of the Great Ones Above whom we name not, my friend Garamond cannot accuse me. My person is sacrosanct. In his ignorance, Mr. Gray has done sacrilege unspeakable, but because he has done this in the pursuit of the law of the Empire, I accord him my forgiveness. But he must not so err again."

Garamond discreetly elbowed his way back. "The Venga Avest has a secret that—"

"My friends," Kennes stepped forward—and in front of Garamond.

"My friends, is this man to disclose the sacred secrets of a holy servant of the precincts of Corbo to the uninitiated?"

"He sure is," Fettle spoke up, grinning wickedly. "Where were you when he wanted to disclose *my* secrets?"

"And mine?" Dheloris echoed. The source of their quarrel now vanished, she and Fettle darted melting glances at one another unabashedly. Their secret would never be secret again, but in hopes that it wouldn't matter terribly, they felt at peace with the world. Enough at peace to poke fun at a Venga Avest.

Lady Maudelaine, for her part, put her hand to her lips and waited in suspense.

Garamond stepped nimbly in front of Kennes, almost landing in Dheloris' lap. "This man is not the Venga Avest of Corbo. This is the agent of the Provincial Governor of Kettlewharf, here investigating the case of the purloined letter. If he has been in holy orders, I have never heard of it."

The guests looked from Kennes to Lady Maudelaine, whom they expected would have revealed him immediately, and back.

Lady Maudelaine stood and addressed Kennes. Unable to step in front of Garamond, Kennes stepped closer to the governor's daughter. He feared this was a dangerous move.

"Kennes, Gaust Kennes," Maudelaine said, "you may wonder why I kept your secret since you came here. You see, I had never seen you before—the real you: forceful, authoritative, stern, yet forgiving. I think you could serve my father as well as spiritual mentor and household priest as you have as agent. Come back to us. And I say *us* because—because I love you."

"That," said Kennes, "is a laudable sentiment. The bestowal of affection is smiled upon by the Great Ones. I, myself, in fact harbour that tender sentiment in my heart, and as the Guardians of the Precinct of Corbo are not forbidden to take such wives as are suitable in the eyes of the Great Ones, I, here before these witnesses, tender unto you, my adored Maudelaine, my proposal of eternal union."

Lady Maudelaine coloured prettily, took his hand, and vowed, "I accept."

"I say," reminded Fettle, who had appointed himself unofficial gadfly, "this chap might be this lady's sweetie-pie, but that doesn't keep him from being a suspect in a murder case."

Kennes stepped yet closer to Lady Maudelaine, and the two looked their defiance on the world.

"True," agreed Garamond. "Although he says he spent that time searching for the parchment, I have no proof of it. Certainly he didn't find it. No, like his lady and like Siphuncle, Kennes is not cleared. None of these three can be cleared until one is proved to be the culprit."

None of the three seemed prepared to make a confession. Kennes and Maudelaine looked tenderly at one another. Siphuncle, who might be suspected of harboring ill feelings at the loss of Maudelaine, showed signs of relief once the girl accepted Kennes' proposal. Not naturally the marrying sort, in spite of some momentary sentiments in that direction at weak moments, Siphuncle felt profound relief at having escaped a lady who might have taken advantage of any weak moments on his part.

Garamond brought the meeting to order, a meeting that had become disgracefully sentimental. "With no confessions on hand, we must take another tack. Now, how did Svarabakti know that the parchment was here? We have her recorded words showing that she did indeed know its location. She hadn't found the letter. If she had, she would have taken it, and very likely sent it off to her superiors in the Fausta. I found it where Yotu found it—and before he moved it. Lord Roderick had hidden it, with considerable presence of mind, in the Scroll Room, a room entirely papered with and given over to displays of congratulatory scrolls, all in the gold and purple of the Shardé Native Chief's latest aesthetic affectation.

"How did she learn it was here? Yotu seems to have wanted to keep it for the use of the Separatists. He might have mentioned it to her, but that seems unlikely. Very possibly she heard of it when Lord Roderick made the call to Lady Maudelaine and requested that she bring it from her father's house—without telling her father. Would you like to explain this, Lady Maudelaine?"

"If you must know, dear Roddy called me up and said he was awfully concerned about the Commonwealth Ceremonies going off all right. He asked me if the Separatists were up to any dirty work. I told him papa and Gaust"—she fluttered her lashes at

Gaust Kennes—"were making hush-hush talky-talk over a purple parchment. He said I must bring it out to him directly, and say nothing about it to papa, 'cause the fate of the Empire depended on it."

Gwen and Garamond nodded *I told you so* to each other. "Lord Roderick," Garamond asked, "have you anything to say?"

Usher drew breath feebly and replied with dignity, "I don't believe I have anything to answer for in that matter."

"Now," Garamond continued, "we know that Lord Roderick called Lady Maudelaine, discussed a Separatist document, and requested that she bring it to him. If Svarabakti overheard this conversation, she would realize that Lord Roderick—but probably not Lady Maudelaine—would know the final hiding place of the document. Since she could not find it, as we know because she didn't find it, she might have gone to the one person who knew where it was to demand it. She could bargain for it because she could expose the person who had it as having stolen an official interplanetary document with full knowledge of the implications of its message."

Lord Roderick once more took out his sodden handkerchief and pressed it to his temples.

35

The room thrilled with anticipation and with a certainty that Garamond was moving toward a momentous conclusion.

Garamond stooped for a moment to give his host a clean handkerchief and to adjust his bandage. He spent rather more time on the bandage that seemed necessary, and once or twice Usher winced away from his touch. When Garamond rose, he asked rhetorically, "What if Svarabakti went to her host and tried to blackmail the parchment from him? To answer that, I ask another question—of the kitchen maid. Miss, when you had disposed of the bristlefish, what did you do with the knife and plate?"

The girl paled, stammered, and finally admitted, "I—I put the fish plate under the egg plate. I daredn't hide it with the fish bones, 'cause they'd count the plates at kitchen and maybe think I broke it. And I left the knife on the tray too, under the edge of the mat a bit. I was very wrong, sir, but . . . but that's what I did, and I wish I'd told sooner, it's been such a torment to me, but I was that a-scared, sir, that someone would think his lordship—"

"That his lordship had used it to stab Svarabakti, miss?" Garamond finished for her. He turned and asked gently, "Lord Roderick, did you use that knife to stab Svarabakti?"

With an effort, Usher pulled himself higher on his cushions. His pallor and his bandages contrasted startlingly with his dark, gossamer hair and feverish dark eyes. "Yes! Yes, but . . ."

The guests gasped, clutching their brows or their hearts, or making whatever dramatic gestures they were accustomed to use to depict astonishment and distress. The kitchen maid screamed. Borcubast staggered and leaned on the kitchen maid for support. The cook considered fainting, but realized she might miss something, and compensated by fanning herself extravagantly with her apron.

Lord Roderick whispered again, "But . . ."

Garamond spoke for him, so everyone could hear, "But she was dead already? Is that what you were going to say?"

"Yes."

"And how, Lord Roderick, did she die, without the serving maid and footman in the hall outside hearing anything or seeing her enter? No, wait"—this to Usher. "You, Brennu," Garamond addressed the footman. "How well do you know the serving maid, Marli?"

"Quite well, sir."

"Very well?"

"Very well, sir."

"And do you like her company?"

"Yes, sir."

"And Marli, do you enjoy Brennu's company?"

"Yes, sir."

"Do you two enjoy each other's company enough to take a moment's well-earned rest in a quiet spot together?"

"Sometimes, sir."

"Yes indeed, sir."

"Enough that yesterday morning you might have gone into the octagonal room across the hall from Usher's bedroom, a very quiet place and convenient for not being overheard. And might you have lost track of time in kissing and canoodling?"

"Oh, save us!" Marli exclaimed. "Was that only yesterday? So much happened with the murder and all, and we have nipped into that room more than once, just for a rest ye understand, sir. I never remembered it was yesterday."

Brennu broke in, "And us perjurin' ourselves over a bit of slap and tickle, as we forgot about shortly, which ain't right. Well, sir, it won't happen again."

Marli looked alarmed.

"I say," Garamond expostulated, "anyone can forget a trivial incident, and it's little disgrace to forget something minor on a day so full of incident." The two nodded. "So that bit of inadvertent false evidence, now that you've amended it, is no reason the two of you shouldn't meet from time to time, though it would perhaps be better out of working hours."

"Oh, no, sir," Brennu corrected. "I don't mean it's the kissin' as won't happen again, it's the forgettin' about it. Kissin' Marli is no trivial incident, sir, as ye would know if ye was myself, but unless ye was myself, ye wouldn't get a chance. It was very wrong of us to give false witness, as innocent as we was in our forgettin'. So to prevent us makin' some likewise mistake in the futuremost time, I guess Marli could see her way to marryin' the chap as most values her kisses."

"That's very pretty talk, Brennu," Marli returned, mock-affronted, "but if a chap values my kisses, what for does he forget 'em? I'd marry the chap as kissed sweetest, I would, and I'll try to figure which chap that is while these people finish their investygation, for as I always says, 'tis business before pleasure, and if murdering is more pleasuresome than marryin', I've never heard of it." The maid and footman subsided smugly into their seats.

Garamond urged Usher delicately, "Perhaps you should explain what actually occurred."

Lord Roderick's voice grew stronger as he recounted, almost with relief, the events of the previous day. "Yes, Svarabakti came to me, furious as only she could be. I had seen her in one argument that morning in my room, when she threw a bronze statuette at Siphuncle. Judging from what I've heard this evening, she had at least two other arguments before she came back to my chamber.

"She must have come in while the servants were across the hall. She didn't make enough noise to attract their attention—she didn't scream, she only hissed, the viper she was. Undoubtedly she didn't want Yotu—or anyone else—to hear her mention the parchment, as she had overheard me. I told her I wouldn't give it up for any bribe or threat. I was lying on the couch near the window where I had been watching the practice for the revelry. I was in a certain amount of pain and may have spoken sharper than I meant, but after all, she was speaking blackmail and treason in the same breath.

"When I refused, she struck me. Lying ill as I was, she struck me across the face with those claws she had. Beast! Beast and coward. The moment she struck me, weak as she knew I was, she leaped back, as if she expected me to beat her. Me!

"When she backed away she tripped. If ever there was poetic justice, it happened then. The statuette she had thrown at Siphuncle had spines that stuck into a snowstone tabletop. She fell back against it before I even realized she was in any danger. She struck her head so hard that by the time I got to her side, she was dead.

"You asked how I could have taken her to the chapel without the servants in the hall knowing. Not simply because they were busy across the hall. They would have heard an exhausted man struggling with the corpse of a tall woman if I had entered the hall with it.

"I didn't. Perhaps Borcubast mentioned the subterranean passageway by which I can go quickly and privately to the chapel?"

Garamond shuddered.

"Ah, he showed it to you. It was fortunate we didn't meet. A door behind a tapestry in my room opens onto a spiral staircase. I dragged the corpse in a sheet behind me. I hadn't the strength to carry it. I barely had the strength to do what I did do. You see now why I was so much weaker yesterday afternoon than the blow of that stone would account for, and why you wondered whether I had been exaggerating my symptoms."

Lord Roderick paused, closed his eyes painfully, and asked for water. Brennu, in the way of Kulmar servants who know what's best, contrary to orders, proffered a tankard of hot cyder. Usher savoured the warmth thankfully.

"I had planned to take her into the mourning room. That would have been fitting to some degree. By the time I brought the corpse up the steps to the chapel, I hardly had the strength to go farther. I hoped the saints would forgive it when I laid her out on their altar. She looked decorative and dramatic, and I thought in my feverish state that she might have appreciated that. I brought the knife along simply to confuse the issue. When I saw what an artistic tableau she made, I realized that the engraved hilt at her breast would add the final touch. As I said, I was feverish. I forgot the garnet necklace. I wouldn't have left anything that pointed falsely to a specific person—in this case to Lady Maudelaine—if I had noticed it. I dragged my way back to my couch, nearly fainting. I don't know how long I lay there before Borcubast came in and announced the death. It didn't seem long at all."

"I see," Garamond returned noncommittally. "Borcubast, when you went to Lord Roderick's room to announce the death, did you see anything different there? Different from when you told Marli and Brennu that he wasn't to be disturbed?"

"Well now, the breakfast tray was still there, on account no one could ha' taken it away without goin' in. And that nasty, spiky statue thing, as Svarabakti threw at Siphuncle, it was gone."

Usher muttered, "I concealed it in a dark corner down in the passageway. I hoped to go back before too long and throw it in the tarn."

"And, sir," Borcubast brightened, "his lordship had a white strip of bandage on his head, as wasn't there before. Up till then, his head had been painin' him, but he only had a sling to his arm, and nothin' on his head. Now he had this bandage-like."

"I put it on," Lord Roderick explained, "before I took the body down. Her nails had cut into me, and I needed to stop the bleeding."

"I . . . Gwen thought as much," Garamond agreed. "When I touched your bandage a few minutes ago, you winced as if from a sharp cut, not a dull bruise. I assume your arm isn't broken. You could hardly have done what you did with the pain of a broken arm. You never could have lifted that weight one-armed."

"No, I think the stone only grazed my head as it fell. Most of its force cut into my arm and bruised it quite painfully."

"And the webwire found where the stone fell? Was it a trap?"

"I don't know. I don't think so. Svarabakti probably dropped it trying to help me up. She was trying so hard to flirt enough to get the attention of a half-conscious man, she could easily have overlooked a bit of wire. No, that's rude of me. She lived her own way, and died the way she lived."

"Perhaps the best epitaph she deserves," Garamond agreed. "Now, though, can you consent to having the authorities come out here? If your story is true, they can do any number of things to confirm it. Match the cuts on your cheek to her nails, match the wounds on her head to the bronze. Check the angle of her fall. Check to be certain she hadn't set a trap for you in the arch to the wine cellar. Will you let them come?"

"I will." Lord Roderick sat up, a good deal of his colour restored. "Yes, I will."

"That reminds me," Brennu spoke up. "Beggin' Yer Lordship's pardon, but that repeatin' of 'I will,' reminds me of a matter of marryin' I hadn't finished with a certain young lady. I'd like her answer in front of all these fine people if it's yes, and I'd like 'em to witness how poor an excuse she has if it's no. So, Marli, what do you say to exchangin' rings in his lordship's chapel, to take the chill off it, like?"

"Why, Mr. Brennu." Marli feigned surprise. "Such a bashful chap as kissed a girl behind the arras for three years and never so much as mentioned rings, and now ye make public announcements afore folks as shouldn't give us more notice than a tea tray. But seein' they've been patient with yer way of askin' the question, I won't make 'em wait longer for the answer, which is yes, Mr. Brennu, I will. Though it's a curious thing, at a 'vestygation of treason and murder, as how Fettle and Dheloris has admitted they's married, and Lady Maudelaine said yes to the Bendy Abest, and we up and engage ourselves. I wonder if there's any others likewise inclined?"

"Now that you mention it," said Yotu, who had been sitting rather dejectedly under the watchful eyes of four sentries, "Yin, silver blossom of the revolution—not but that we may have to await further hopes of revolution in vile incarceration—would it brighten your days of captivity to know I not only share them, but share your love?"

"That is a delightful sentiment, friend and instigator of riot. Let us wed, and then if we are shot at dawn, though I very much hope otherwise, we will be a romantic memory to inspire insurrection and coups d'état."

"Anyone else?" Garamond asked uneasily. "Siphuncle, do you perhaps hanker after the kitchen maid?"

"Not really, old fellow." Siphuncle brushed up his beard thoughtfully. "I hanker more for a bit of freedom, new tribal musics to run through my guitar, and romance to have where I find it—and to leave when it withers for me or for she. No offense, of course, to the kitchen maid, I hope, miss."

"No, sir, not at all, sir." The thought of all this marrying had brought out the tripling's handkerchee afresh, but she quivered on the brink on a momentous decision, and in a moment, decided. "Borcubast, sir, ye've been nice to me and picked me up when I fainted, and let me cry on ye, and lent me handkerchees. Well, neither of us is goin' to get proposals from real glamorous folks, and I figure as how if I know I have a friend forever, I won't need so many handkerchees, nor have never so many faintin's or screamin's, which I think triplings is bound to do 'cause not many has anyone to marry with.

"So if you could see yer way to pledgin' with me in chapel, I'd be a friend to ye, and moreso, if ye take my meanin'."

Borcubast took her meaning and took her hand, but something must have gotten in his eye, as he had to borrow her handkerchee back rather hastily.

"Anyone more?" Garamond looked around warily. "We'd better get our host back to a warm bed and rest, and prepare for a late dinner for us all, before we collapse on the spot."

"Garamond, aren't you forgetting someone?" Gwen said brightly.

"Oh, sorry. Kelesophos and Patrice? Do you want to add to this matrimonial merriment?"

"Only to say"—Patrice grinned, fluffing her hair lavishly—"that we settled on a wedding date while we were grubbing under Yotu's bed looking for incriminating vid discs. Perhaps we should thank you, Yotu, for giving us the opportunity."

Yotu bowed but with limited enthusiasm.

"Garamond, that wasn't what I meant at all," Gwen reminded. "After all, we've been kissing cousins since—well, you know when since. Isn't it time we stop being cousins and cross a couple of twigs on the old family tree? Easier than grafting, they say."

"Actually..." Garamond realized that his collar had grown amazingly tight. "Actually, I had thought we should wait another year. I say, Siphuncle, if you were in my position, you'd wait another year, wouldn't you?"

Siphuncle stroked his beard. "Now if you, Gwen, were the running-off-with sort of lady, I would take great pleasure in running off with you. But seeing that the marriage mania has struck, if I were in Garamond's position, I would indeed give you a long, soulful look, and suggest another year."

"There, now." Garamond brightened. "It's not entertaining for all these people to listen to us quarrel, so another year it must be. After all, you always say I need practice."

"I . . . what!" Gwen looked around for something to throw, thought better of it, and promised, "I'll get even for this. When this year's up, just see if I don't."

36

Garamond cleared his throat and stooped over his host. "I say, hadn't we better get you back to your room? Here, lie still and some of the chaps can carry you up on this couch."

Brennu hurried forward with some of his cronies to assist.

"Still," Garamond added, and his listeners groaned, "I have another question. You, Brennu, and Marli, can hardly have neglected your duties as long as it took Lord Roderick to do what he did. Yet you say you heard him the whole while—the whole time you were listening, we understand now. You even heard him rustling the papers on his desk, something he never mentioned. Whom could you have heard? You saw no one enter—but then, you didn't see Svarabakti go in."

"I don't know who it could be, sir, but he didn't have no right among his lordship's papers." Brennu looked suspiciously about him. "It wouldn't be that Yotu, would it?"

Yotu, incensed, replied shortly, "No, it wouldn't."

Lord Roderick looked up, puzzled. "It wasn't I. I had no time or strength for papers that day."

"Up, then." Garamond directed the footmen to lift the couch. "We shall see." He led the way, and paused a moment at the door to ask Kelesophos, "Did the rinds work?"

Kelesophos nodded, grinning.

Most of the servants melted away. As spacious as it was, Lord Roderick's suite of rooms would hardly hold a fraction of his staff in any comfort. Four of the sentries escorted Yotu down the subterranean passageways, where they locked him in a well-built dungeon cell, dating from the days when the manor had been a Vonyushar fortress. Then, too, Shardé Separatists had risen against their overlords as they did today, and the Vonyushar peace keepers had found three-meter-thick stone walls effective in quieting their traitorous propaganda.

At the door of Lord Roderick's room, Garamond had Usher's couch put down in the hall, and signalled for silence. Anyone could hear the subdued shufflings and restless groaning within. In the presence of as many witnesses as could crowd into view, Garamond opened the door. Within, a bright-plumaged pootock and a perky poot hen groaned in imitation of the sound they most often heard from outside Usher's window. They uttered their hypocritical groans as they pecked busily and bright-eyed at the candied rinds Kelesophos had left on a table for them, and preened the last of the rainwater out of their feathers.

"I remember now." Lord Roderick, enlightened, explained: "I had left the window open to watch the revelings before Svarabakti entered. When I came back after I . . . had been to the chapel, I saw a pootock fly out. I thought nothing of it at the time. My, but I feel better now. It's as if the whole house were at ease now that the mysteries are solved."

As the footmen stowed Usher carefully in his bed, Hyota-ya evicted the pootocks, thoughtfully putting the remainder of the rinds on the balcony for their dining enjoyment. "Why, look," he exclaimed. "The storm is over. Even a few stars are showing between the clouds. And listen. The little voices, the spirits of the house, are grateful. The arguing and hating and fighting and sneaking are over, and they are glad."

"What do you mean, Hyota-ya?" asked Lord Roderick. "I have always fancied that the house had a sentience or a presiding spirit, but I thought only I could hear its voice. Sometimes I wondered whether I was losing my reason. Sometimes it plagued me with questions, sometimes it wafted oppressive doubts around me. It is something I do not understand."

"I hear them more clearly now." Hyota-ya leaned on the window ledge. "Tiny, high whispers. With your sensitive hearing, Lord Roderick, I can see how you would have heard when the others only felt hints of it. But what is it?" The Shardé moved his head back and forth around the window, turning to give his ears full play. "Why, it might be the funguses." He laughed. "They say yes. A vast communal fungus with a highly developed nervous system—it's not impossible. The tendrils reach here and there throughout the manor, listening, guessing, whispering. They seem to be Loyalists, by their views. No wonder Yin thought that they were evil spirits. Perhaps they have adopted your politics."

"Wait," Gwen interrupted. "You never told us, Lord Roderick, why you had Lady Maudelaine bring the parchment to you. Kennes"—the Venga Avest bowed—"said you had said it would be valuable to the Fausta or the Separatists. But if you're a Loyalist, why would you . . .?"

"Would I sell it or use it for blackmail?" Lord Roderick stretched contentedly in his bed. "No, not at all. As Lady Maudelaine mentioned, I called her up to see if the Separatists were planning any obstruction to the Commonwealth Ceremonies. As you've seen, I have my heart set on bringing my friends to add to the pageantry of the celebrations. When I heard that a letter existed that might spoil my plans—and incidentally shake the foundations of the Empire—I, pardon my officiousness, didn't trust the governor to handle the matter properly. I thought the parchment would be safer in my home.

"The warnings I gave the governor were just that—warnings against the terrible consequences that could befall if the parchment were in less safe hands than mine. How could I guess that in his panic he would take them as threats, as blackmail? How could I know that one of my own guests—and an artist of note—could be a traitor to the Empire, to his own chief, and to the prevailing political fashion?

"I'm glad to think that our revelry will enliven the Commonwealth festivities with no Separatist interruption—and without Yotu's abominable violin."

That night, after a toothsome, if late, supper, Gwen and Garamond flew back to Kettlewharf in Lord Roderick's air car, chauffeured by Brennu. They carried the purple parchment, and a gram to the governor from Kennes who "requested leave to remain, confirming curious elements of the investigation." Since the burgeoning love between himself and Lady Maudelaine could be called a curious element, his message had some truth to it.

Around midnight, with a minimum of fuss and bother, the Kettlewharf contingent of the Peace Office arrived at the Usher mansion and departed at dawn with Yotu and Yin. With them they took Svarabakti's body for the coroner's entertainment. They obtained the knife, the bronze statuette, and an exhaustively detailed simulacrum of the mansion. They took statements from everyone, even the little kitchen maid, who held Borcubast's hand throughout and never shed a tear nor wept a weep. On the basis of these statements, the Peace Office determined that Lord Roderick and his guests need not be detained for the time being, but must stay in the area to give evidence at Yotu's trial. Since everyone had intended to stay with Usher until the month-end, this caused no inconvenience whatsoever.

Celebration

Being the Epilogue
in which Virtue Is Rewarded

The ceremonies at month-end to celebrate the entry of Shardworld into the Oriel-Mossmarching Empire almost equalled Lord Roderick's ambitious fancies. To crown it all, the Empress came in person: Her Puissant Imperial Majesty, Gloriana Gladiola, Empress of Oriel-Mossmarching, with so many titles after that as to quite exhaust the livried Oriel Pursuivant Herald who announced them.

Lord Roderick and his guests noted that the Empress indeed had a face rather like a biscuit, not to mention a body like dumpling, and, as was her wont, crowned her kindly, if unlovely, features with a hat extravagantly arrayed with mauve plumes. She beamed and blinked and puttered about in a dignified fashion precisely like a Palomedes puff pigeon. The people adored her.

The revelries planned by Lord Roderick enlivened the ceremonies no end. Whatever fears of mad assassins kept him in his guarded manor, they dissipated at the thought of participating in public pageantry. Kelesophos' dudelsack squealed tooth-shatteringly, the fourth trumpeteer invented some remarkable discords, the flowers wilted, and the stately gray-haired actor accidentally trod on Patrice's skirt. The Empress, used to amateur entertainments throughout the Empire, declared herself enchanted.

Lord Roderick presented the Imperial Grand Panjandrum with a gold and purple scroll that he had drawn up all by himself—rather uneven in the lettering—expressing his continued pleasure in service to the Empire. It enclosed a princely denomination of treasury note—the denomination with the portrait of Prince Walter. It had been to this scroll that Usher had referred, quite alarming Lady Maudelaine with the mention of publicly handing it to the Grand Panjandrum.

At the end of a day of exhausting merriment, the Empress, flanked by the Provincial Governor of Kettlewharf, the Shardé Native Chief, a number of lesser governors, the Grand Panjandrum, and a full complement of seven heralds, bestowed patents of arms, grants of arms, and other awards primarily of interest to heralds, journalists, and the recipients. To crown it all, the Vert Manche Herald, with two green silken sleeves to his purple tunic, announced the presentation of a knighthood.

The populace, beginning to drowse in folding chairs in the spacious but now much bedraggled Hoyataho-o Park, sat up and took notice. No one on Shardworld had ever received knighthood. (Sir Cargyle, the governor, had gotten his as governor of Upper Ploughdog.) Thus would the Empire reward Shard for ceasing its revolutions and gracefully permitting the Empire to absorb it.

Lord Roderick Usher had no doubt who would receive the accolade. His eloquent scroll, and its yet more eloquent contents, surely merited such award.

The Shardé Native Chief smiled the nonchalant smile of one pretending to wonder to whom the Oriel spurs and Mossmarching crimson sash would be bestowed. Those who knew him might have seen a betraying quiver in his tail and cheek tufts, as he sat arrayed as his conception of a Roman emperor, hoping his purple toga would not clash with the sash.

Inspector General Carp also smiled nonchalantly.

A tremendous crisis had been averted. He had seen a particular scroll burned. True, the acts of others had brought this about, but everyone knew that the mere threat of his actions had set those others scurrying. He had always rather fancied spurs. As a knight, he might obtain a riding stag so he could show his off.

The precise sentiments of Inspector General Carp also quickened the pulse of Gaust Kennes. His brilliant planning had prompted the action of others. Further, as the Venga Avest of Shard and spiritual advisor (as well as agent) to His Excellency the governor, he felt his spurs almost divinely ordained.

The Grays eyed each other warily. If two knighthoods were to be bestowed upon close relations, they would have been announced at one time. The Vert Manche Herald gave no sign that more than one knighthood would be given. Confident in their works, the Grays remembered the parchment burned and Yin and Yotu incarcerated. (The traitorous Shardé had to make the scrolls for the Empress' awards to the loyal heroes.) No flaws could the cousins find in their pursuit of the investigation—but one knighthood between them? To whom would it go?

True, the Empress had admitted them into the Loyal Legion of the Golden Hippogriff for unarmed aid in time of undeclared insurrection, but who more than they deserved this accolade?

The ceremony took precisely long enough to build proper suspense and allow a number of the onlookers to hope for the award. If they didn't get it now, the logic ran, they would work the harder for it next time—after they stopped sulking.

Vert Manche Herald cleared his throat. A breeze off the sea brought the scent of fisheries and canneries and kelp harvests— the sweet scent of commerce. The Imperial Trumpeter blew a fanfare so clear and sweet, so intricate with grace notes and flourishes, as to spur Lord Roderick on to greater musical ambitions.

Vert Manche shook his green sleeves of office and announced, "Her Puissant Imperial Majesty Gloriana Gladiola calls forward into the glorious ranks of the Order of the Knights of the Bengal Bangle" (commemorating a relic of a battlefield of Old Earth) "one esteemed citizen of the Shardé world who has aided nobly in averting discord and crisis, in bringing traitors to justice, in the discreet investigation of diplomatic emergencies" (thus the speech writers described the death of a famed and flamboyant singer in the mansion of an Imperial ambassador) "and in the discovery of a new sentient lifeform—make way for Sir Hyota-ya!" The audience, led by the Shardé natives, erupted into a standing ovation.

The Grays sighed, shrugged, and hugged. Lady Maudelaine kissed Kennes under her father's nose, but the governor made no complaint. Kelesophos and Patrice nearly strangled their Shardé friend in a three-way congratulatory embrace. The Empress adjusted her appalling hat, the crowd cheered her for 7.3 standard minutes (Kelesophos won a wage as to the length of the applause), and the Oriel Pursuivant signalled the governor's household staff to clear away the chairs for dancing.

The closing cliché in the chronicle of the festivities as written by the lead reporter of the *Kettlewharf Clarion*, "A good time was had by all," came remarkably near to the truth.

Appendix

Limericks

From *An Anthology of Fetlocks*, by Fettle of Froschtower, published by Fetteloris Press, Froschtower, Hohenheim.

p. 85

The Venga at breakfast on Shard
Found his eggs had been flavoured with lard.
It's not that they stick
To his lips when they lick,
But he fancies the flavour is marred.

p. 145

The door guards at Lord Roddy's castle
Attempted to give me a hassle.
I soon set them straight
With a blow to the pate
And snatched off their helms by the tassle.

p. 151

Svarabakti, once brimming with life,
Met her end on a bristlefish knife.
The rotter who slayed her
And nearly filleted her
Understood she'd be no patient wife.

ATANIELLE ANNYN NOËL grew up on an isolated cattle ranch rich in granite and chaparral in Southern California. San Diego State University first introduced her to other people of her age who openly admitted to recreational reading, to whom Jane Austen suggested something besides a dress boutique and Dickens conveyed more than a mild oath. After twelve years of cloistered academe, she was graduated with honors, a Masters in Education, and a dog-eared copy of *Pride and Prejudice*.

Ms. Noël now lives on a small remnant of the family ranch in an adobe house so rustic it has been mistaken for a refurbished stagecoach station, where she reads, draws, gardens, and benignly defaces reams of writing paper. Her first novel, also set in the Oriel-Mossmarching Empire, was *The Duchess of Kneedeep*.